# LIFE FORM

Amélie Nothomb

# LIFE FORM

*Translated from the French
by Alison Anderson*

Europa
*editions*

Europa Editions
214 West 29th Street
New York, N.Y. 10001
www.europaeditions.com
info@europaeditions.com

Copyright © 2010 by Éditions Albin Michel
First Publication 2013 by Europa Editions

Translation by Alison Anderson
Original title: *Une forme de vie*
Translation copyright © 2012 by Europa Editions

Library of Congress Cataloging in Publication Data is available
ISBN 978-1-60945-088-5

Nothomb, Amélie
Life Form

Book design by Emanuele Ragnisco
www.mekkanografici.com

Cover photo © Sarah Moon

Prepress by Grafica Punto Print – Rome

Printed in the USA

# LIFE FORM

That morning I received a new sort of letter:

*Baghdad, December 18, 2008*

Dear Amélie Nothomb,

I'm a private in the US Army, my name is Melvin Mapple, you can call me Mel. I've been posted in Baghdad ever since the beginning of this fucking war, over six years ago. I'm writing to you because I am as down as a dog. I need some understanding and I know that if anyone can understand me, you can.

Please answer. I hope to hear from you soon.

Melvin Mapple

At first I thought this was some sort of hoax. Even if Melvin Mapple did exist, what right did he have to speak to me like that? Wasn't there some sort of military censorship to prevent words like "fucking" from being used in conjunction with "war?"

I took a closer look at the letter. If it was a fake, it was a remarkably good one. The stamp was American, the postmark Iraqi. The most authentic thing about it was the handwriting, that basic American script, simple, stereotypical, that I had noticed so often on my visits to the United

States. And the tone of the letter, so direct, indisputably legitimate.

When I was no longer in doubt as to the authenticity of the missive, I was struck by what was the most incredible aspect of the message: while there might be nothing surprising about the fact that an American soldier, caught up in the war right from the start, said he was "as down as a dog," it was completely mind-boggling that he would write to me about it.

How had he come to hear of me? A few of my novels, five years or so ago, had been translated into English and garnered a, shall we say, rather intimate readership. As for soldiers, Belgian and French ones had written to me, there was nothing surprising about that; more often than not they were asking for a photograph with a dedication. But a private in the US Army, based in Iraq? That was beyond me.

Did he know who I was? Other than the fact that my publisher's address was spelled correctly on the envelope, there was no proof that he did. "I need some understanding and I know that if anyone can understand me, you can." How could he be so sure that I would understand him? Assuming he had read my books, were they any sort of solid proof of human compassion and understanding? I could not help but be puzzled by Melvin Mapple's choice of wartime pen pal.

Moreover, did I really want to have him confide in me? There were already so many people who wrote to me at great length about their troubles. My capacity for putting up with other people's pain was fit to burst. What's more, the suffering of an American soldier would take up a lot of room. Did I have that sort of space? No.

Melvin Mapple must have been in need of a shrink.

That's not my job. I would not be doing him any favors by allowing him to confide in me, because he'd think he no longer needed the kind of therapy that six years of war surely warranted.

But not to reply at all would have been a low-down rotten thing to do. I decided on a compromise: I autographed some dedicated copies of my books that had been translated into English to the soldier, put them in a parcel, and sent them off. That way I felt like I'd done my duty by this US Army underling, and my conscience was at ease.

Some time later it occurred to me that the lack of censorship might be explained by Barack Obama's recent election to the presidency; although it was true he wouldn't be taking office for at least another month, this upheaval must already be having a certain impact. Obama had been a constant, vocal opponent to the war, and had clearly stated that in the event of a Democratic victory he would bring the troops home. I had a vision of Melvin Mapple's imminent return to his native land: in my dreams he would return to his cozy farm surrounded by cornfields, and his parents would be standing there with their arms spread wide. This thought was enough to calm me altogether. And as he would surely take my signed books home with him, I would have done my bit, however indirectly, to promote reading in the Corn Belt.

N ot even two weeks had gone by when I received
Private Mapple's reply:

*Baghdad, January 1, 2009*

Dear Amélie Nothomb,

Thank you for your novels. What do you want me to do
with them?
Happy New Year,

Melvin Mapple

I thought this was a bit much. Slightly annoyed, I wrote
back right away:

*Paris, January 6, 2009*

Dear Melvin Mapple,

I don't know. Perhaps you can use them to balance a
piece of furniture or raise up a chair leg. Or give them to
a friend who has just learned how to read.
Thank you for your new year's wishes. Same to you.

Amélie Nothomb

I mailed the note, fulminating against my stupidity. How else had I expected a soldier to react?

He wrote back right away:

*Baghdad, January 14, 2009*

Dear Amélie Nothomb,

Sorry, I must not have made myself very clear. What I meant was, if I wrote to you it was because I have already read your books, all of the ones in English. I didn't want to bother you with that, that's why I didn't mention them; it went without saying. But I'm glad to have the extra copies, all signed on top of it. I can lend them to my buddies. Sorry to have inconvenienced you.

Sincerely,

Melvin Mapple

My eyebrows shot up. This guy had read all my books, and was establishing a relationship of cause and effect between that event and the fact he was writing to me. This plunged me deep into an abyss of thought. I tried to understand what, in my novels, could have incited this soldier to write to me.

On the other hand, this event had transformed me into that ridiculously delighted individual: the author who discovers that someone has read their oeuvre. The fact that this someone was a private in the US Army was even more gratifying. It made me feel as if I were a universal writer. I felt a grotesque surge of pride. In a supremely contented disposition I composed the following epistle:

*Paris, January 20, 2009*

Dear Melvin Mapple,

I do apologize for the misunderstanding. I am genuinely touched that you have read all my books. Allow me to take this opportunity to send you my latest novel translated into English, *Tokyo Fiancée*, which has just been published in the US. The title annoys me, it sounds like a movie with Sandra Bullock, but the publisher assured me that *Ni d'Ève ni d'Adam* was not likely to find a better translation. From the 1st to the 14th of February I will be in your fine country to promote the book.

Today Barack Obama was inaugurated as president of the United States. It is a great day. I imagine you will be home soon and I am glad.

Best wishes,

Amélie Nothomb

While I was on my American tour, I took every opportunity to inform whoever would listen that I was corresponding with a soldier based in Baghdad who had read all my books. This went over really well with the journalists. The *Philadelphia Daily Reporter* entitled their article "US Army Soldier Reads Belgian Writer Amélie Nothomb". I wasn't exactly sure what sort of aura this news item would surround me with, but it seemed to produce an excellent effect.

Back in Paris, a mountain of mail was waiting for me, including two letters from Iraq.

*Baghdad, January 26, 2009*

Dear Amélie Nothomb,

Thank you for *Tokyo Fiancée*. Don't be annoyed, it's a good title. I love Sandra Bullock. I'm looking forward to reading it. I'll have plenty of time, you know: we won't be coming home just yet. The new president said the troop withdrawal would take nineteen months. And you'll see, since I was the first to arrive, I'll be the last to leave: story of my life. But you're right, Barack Obama is the man for the job. I voted for him.

Sincerely,

Melvin Mapple

*Baghdad, February 7, 2009*

Dear Amélie Nothomb,

I loved *Tokyo Fiancée.* I hope Sandra Bullock will agree to play the part, that would be great. What a beautiful story! I cried at the end. I don't need to ask you if it really happened: it's so authentic.

How was your trip to the States?

Sincerely,

Melvin Mapple

I wrote straight back:

*Paris, February 16, 2009*

Dear Melvin Mapple,

I'm glad you liked my book.

I had a good time in your beautiful country. I talked about you wherever I went: look at this article from the *Philadelphia Daily Reporter.* Unfortunately I wasn't able to tell the journalists where you were from. I know so little about you. If you don't mind, do tell me more about yourself.

Best wishes,

Amélie Nothomb

I preferred not to comment on a hypothetical film with Sandra Bullock: I'd said that as a joke, I didn't expect to be taken seriously. Melvin Mapple might be disappointed if he found out the film didn't stand much of a chance of seeing the light of day. Let's not drive the Corn Belt to despair.

*Baghdad, February 21, 2009*

Dear Amélie Nothomb,

I really enjoyed the article in the *Philadelphia Daily Reporter.* I showed it to my buddies, they all want to write to you now. I told them there was no point, that your American tour was already over. All they want is to get their name in the newspaper.

You want me to tell you about myself. I'm thirty-nine years old, I'm one of the oldest at my rank. I went into the army late, when I was thirty, because I didn't have any prospects for the future. I was dying of hunger.

My parents met in 1967, during the famous Summer of Love. They were ashamed when they found out I'd enlisted. I told them that in America when you're dying of hunger, there's nothing else to do. "You could have come and lived with your parents, couldn't you?" they said. I would have been ashamed to go and sponge off my parents, who are barely making ends meet. They live in a suburb outside Baltimore, where they have a gas station. That's where I grew up, I really didn't feel like going back there. Baltimore is no good for anything except rock music. Unfortunately I am not musically talented.

Before I turned thirty I had dreams and ideals, and I tried to fulfill them. I wanted to become the next Kerouac, but no matter how hard I tried to hit the road high on Benzedrine I couldn't write a single decent line. I drowned myself in booze trying to become the next Bukowski, and that's when I hit rock bottom. So, okay, I figured it out: I didn't have what it takes to be a writer. I tried painting: a disaster. Drip painting is not as easy as you think. I wanted to be an actor; I got nowhere there, either. I lived on the street. I'm glad I went through it, sleeping rough. It taught me a lot.

I enlisted in 1999. I told my parents there was no risk, the last war was too recent. My theory was that the Gulf War in 1991 would keep things calm militarily in the US for a good long while. The army in peacetime seemed like a cool idea. Okay, there was stuff going on in Eastern Europe, in Africa, there was still Saddam Hussein in Iraq, but I couldn't see any major conflicts lurking on the horizon. Which just goes to show I don't have much of a head for politics.

Military life wasn't all roses, I found that out right away. All the training, the discipline, the shouting, the schedules, I never liked any of that. But at least I wasn't a bum anymore. That was important. I'd understood my limits: sleeping on the street, cold and afraid, was one of them. Hunger was another.

In the army you can eat. The food is good, there's plenty of it, and it's free. The day I enlisted they weighed me: a hundred and twenty pounds for five foot nine. I don't think I fooled them for one minute as to the real reason I'd joined up. I know I'm for sure not the only one who's ever become a soldier for that reason.

Sincerely,

Melvin Mapple

I'd been way off with the Corn Belt: the suburbs of Baltimore, that was a lot harder. Baltimore: it's not for nothing that the filmmaker John Waters, the king of trash, set all his films there. It was a city that looked like one ugly suburb. So a suburb of Baltimore, I hardly dared imagine what that might be like.

On September 11, 2001, poor Melvin Mapple must have come to realize his mistake. No, it was not a time of peace. He would pay dearly for his hunger.

Dear Melvin Mapple,

Thank you for your very interesting letter. I liked it very much, I feel like I am getting to know you. Don't hesitate to tell me what comes next, or share other aspects of your life with me, as you like.

Best wishes,

Amélie Nothomb

*Baghdad, March 2, 2009*

Dear Amélie Nothomb,

In the army we make a little money. With my salary I've been buying books. By chance I read the first of yours to be translated into English, *The Stranger Next Door.* I was hooked. I got hold of all your books. It's hard to explain, but your books speak to me.

If you knew me better you would understand. My health is deteriorating. I'm very tired.

Sincerely,

Melvin Mapple

This note worried me no end. I imagined all kinds of

reasons to fall ill in Iraq: the toxic substances used by the military, the stress, perhaps a battle wound. But I'd already asked him to tell me about himself, so I couldn't go begging him for more. Was it his health that was holding him back? I thought I sensed a reticence of another order. I did not know what would be the best approach to adopt and I didn't reply. It was just as well. I received another letter:

*Baghdad, March 5, 2009*

Dear Amélie Nothomb,

I'm feeling a bit better, and have found the strength to write to you. Let me explain: I'm suffering from an illness that seems to be more and more common among the American troops in Iraq. Since the beginning of the conflict, the number of patients has doubled and is still growing. Under the Bush administration our pathology was kept hidden, because it was considered degrading for the image of the US Army. Since Obama, the newspapers have started talking about us, but ever so quietly. You'd be justified in assuming it's some sort of venereal disease, but you'd be wrong.

I am obese. And not by nature. As a child and adolescent I was normal. As an adult I got really thin because I was poor. I enlisted in 1999 and very quickly I put on weight, but there was nothing shocking about it: I'd been famished, all skin and bones, and at last I had the chance to eat. In one year I reached my normal weight for a muscular soldier: one hundred and seventy-six pounds. And I stayed there without any effort until the war. In March, 2003, I was part of the first contingent sent to Iraq. The trouble started as soon as I got there. I saw my first combat, with rocket fire, tanks, bodies exploding next to me and the men I killed myself. I discovered the meaning of terror. There may be some brave people who can stand it, but I'm not one of them. Some people lose their appetite, but most of them, including me, have just the opposite reaction. You come back from battle in a state of shock, terrified, amazed that you're alive, and the first thing you do after you change your pants (you'll have soiled them for sure) is make a beeline for the food. To be more exact, you start off with a beer—beer is another thing for fatties. You guzzle down one or two cans and then you reach for something more solid. Hamburgers, fries, peanut butter and jelly sandwiches, apple pie, brownies, ice cream, all you can eat. So you eat. You wouldn't believe how much you can eat. You go crazy. There's something broken in us. It's not exactly that we like eating in this way, we just can't help it, we could kill ourselves eating, and maybe that's what we want. In the beginning some of us threw up. I tried but I never managed. I wish I could have. You're in pain, your belly is about to explode. You swear you'll never do it again, it hurts too bad. Then the next day you have to go back into combat, the atrocities you have to deal with are even worse than the day before, you just can't get used to it, you get these horrible stomach cramps and you're shooting and running all the while, you just want the nightmare to end. The men who make it back are just empty. So you start with the beer and the food again, and your stomach gradually gets so huge that it doesn't hurt anymore. The ones who were vomiting didn't vomit anymore. We all started getting fat as pigs. Every week we had to ask for uniforms the next size up. It was embarrassing, but no one knew how to curb the tendency. And then you start thinking that it's not your body anymore. It's happening to someone else. All this food is getting shoved down someone else's throat. The proof is that you notice it less and less. Which means you can shovel down more and more. It's not pleasure you feel, but a horrible comfort.

I know what pleasure is, and this isn't it. Pleasure is a great thing. Like making love, for example. That won't happen to me anymore. Because who would want to have anything to do with me, for a start. And because I can't do it anymore. How can you move even a fraction with a body that weighs four hundred pounds? Can you imagine, since I've been in Iraq I've put on over two hundred pounds. Forty pounds a year. And it's not over. I'll be here another eighteen months, time enough to put on seventy pounds. That's assuming I stop putting on weight when I get home. Like a lot of American soldiers, I'm a bulimic who can't throw up. In these conditions, losing weight is the last thing imaginable.

Two hundred pounds is already a huge person. I'm richer by one whole huge person now. Since she came and joined me here, I've been calling her Scheherazade. It's not very kind to the real Scheherazade, who must have been a slender creature. But I'd rather identify her with one person and not two, and with a woman rather than a man, probably because I'm heterosexual. Besides, I like the idea of Scheherazade. She speaks to me all night long. She knows I can't make love anymore, so instead of doing it with me she charms me with her beautiful stories. I'll let you in on my secret: it's thanks to Scheherazade's storytelling that I can live with my obesity. I don't need to make you a drawing to show you what would happen to me if the guys found out I gave the name of a woman to my fat. But I know that you won't judge me. You have a few obese characters in your books, and the way you portray them they never lack dignity. And in your books they make up strange legends, like Scheherazade, to be able to go on living.

It's as if she were the one writing this letter. I can't get her to stop. I've never written such a long message in my life, which proves it's not me. I hate my obesity, but I love Scheherazade. At night when my weight presses down my chest, I imagine it's not me but a beautiful young woman lying on my body. I immerse myself in the story and I can hear her sweet feminine voice murmuring indescribable things in my ear. Then my fat arms squeeze her flesh and it's so convincing that instead of feeling my own flab, I am touching a lover's smooth skin. At times like that, believe me, I am happy. Better still: we are happy, she and I, the way only lovers can be.

It's not like it's protecting me from anything: you can die from obesity, it does happen, and since I'm going to go on putting on weight, it will catch up with me sooner or later. But if Scheherazade will have me right to the end, I'll die a happy man. That's all. Scheherazade and I wanted to tell you this story.

Sincerely,

Melvin Mapple

*Paris, March 10, 2009*

Dear Melvin Mapple,

Thank you for this incredible missive of yours, which I have just read and reread with stupefaction and wonder. What you have just told me leaves me speechless. The more I think about it, the more disgusted, amazed, and dazzled I am. May I ask you both, you and Scheherazade, to tell me this story over and over again? I have never read anything like it.

Best wishes,

Amélie Nothomb

I waited feverishly for Melvin's next epistle. I was bombarded with the most extraordinary images: one minute I saw Iraqis being blown to bits, explosions shattering my skull, then a minute later it was American soldiers stuffing their faces so traumatizingly that their bellies were reproducing the explosions on the front line. I could see portliness gaining ground, then defenses lost one after the other as the next size up gradually became indispensable, an entire front line of fat inching its way across the map. The US Army was swelling, growing ever larger, like a gigantic larva absorbing some indistinct substance, maybe its Iraqi victims. One of the military units is the *corps*—which in French means body—and what I was seeing must have been a body, insofar as one can use this word to refer to an efflorescence of fat. Then again, in English, *corpse* means a dead body. In French, that is only one meaning for the word *corps*. Is an obese body a living body? The only proof it has that it is still alive is that it goes on getting fat. Such is the logic of obesity.

Then I imagined someone who might be Melvin Mapple, lying on his back and suffocating in the night. I worked out that of the two hundred pounds he'd put on, the weight located in the chest and belly must represent roughly half: one hundred and ten pounds for

Scheherazade was a credible size, so I could believe in the existence of a lover lying over his heart. And I could picture their idyll, their intimate conversations, the blossoming of love in the place they least expected it. In six years of war there had been well over a thousand and one nights.

We have known, since Pascal, that "he who would act the angel acts the beast." Melvin Mapple was adding his own version: he who would act the beast acts the angel. To be sure, his story was not solely a tale of angelism, far from it. But the power of this vision which enabled my correspondent to endure something so intolerable was deserving of respect.

Among the people who came up to me at the Paris Book Fair to ask me to sign their books was an obese young woman. By then I was so contaminated by Melvin's letters that the young girl seemed almost frail to me, as she nestled in the embrace of the Romeo holding fast to her body.

*Baghdad, March 17, 2009*

Dear Amélie Nothomb,

I was touched by your reaction. But I hope you aren't exaggerating the lyrical side of my situation. You know, even if Obama is president, the war is not over. It won't be over until our opponents think it's over, too. For as long as we're here, we'll be in danger. It's true the terrible assaults that made me bulimic have come to an end. But even a small offensive makes us targets again; there are still soldiers in our ranks who are getting killed. That's because the people here have it in for us, and no doubt they have good reason.

Obese folks like me always get sent to the front. It's pointless for me to explain why, it's dead obvious: a fat man makes the best human shield. A normal body might protect a single individual, but mine protects two or three. Especially as our presence acts as a lightning rod: the Iraqis are so hungry, it's as if our obesity is mocking them, so we're the ones they want to target first and foremost.

I am convinced that the American leaders want the same thing. That's the reason, too, why the obese soldiers are bound to stay here until Obama decides on the final day: to increase the probability of our demise. After every conflict, there have been soldiers suffering from all sorts of abominable pathologies who go home and guilt trip the entire country. But their afflictions were usually so special that the population could always blame them on everything about war that surpasses human understanding.

Obesity, on the other hand, is nothing peculiar in America, it's just pathetic. Although it is a disease, most ordinary folk rarely view it as one, and they talk about us in terms that imply we're still doing all right. The US Army can put up with a lot, except being grotesque. "You had a rough time? It doesn't look like it!" or "What else did you do in Iraq besides eat?" are the sort of remarks we'll be met with. We're in for a real hard time with public opinion. The US Army thinks it's imperative to project a virile image of brute strength and courage. But with our obesity we've been landed with enormous breasts and buttocks, and that projects a female image of softness and cowardice.

The corporals tried to put us on a diet. No way: our gluttony has made us capable of anything. Food is a drug like any other and it is easier to deal doughnuts than coke. They imposed a period of food prohibition on us but we only got even fatter than under normal circumstances. Once they lifted the embargo on food our weight gain went right back to cruising speed.

Let's talk about drugs, while we're at it: modern warfare is unbearable without drugs. In Vietnam our boys had opium, and say what you like about it, it's not nearly as habit-forming as my own addiction to pastrami sandwiches. When the boys got home in the sixties and seventies, none of them went on with their opium habit— opium's pretty hard to come by in the States. When we go home, how are we supposed to wean ourselves off junk food when you can find it anywhere? Our leaders would have done better to hand out the opium, at least we wouldn't be obese now. Food is the most harmful, addictive drug there is.

They say you're supposed to eat to live. Well, we're eating to die. It's the only form of suicide we have at our disposal. We're so enormous that we hardly seem human, and yet the most human guys among us are the ones who have foundered in overeating. Some guys can put up with the monstrosity of war without ever getting sick. I don't admire them. That's not bravery, it's a lack of sensitivity on their part.

There were no weapons of mass destruction in Iraq. And even supposing there were some doubts on the matter, there's no doubt anymore. The whole conflict has been a scandalous injustice. I'm not trying to exonerate myself. I might be less guilty than George W. Bush and his gang, but I'm guilty all the same. I took part in the horror, I killed soldiers, I killed civilians. I blew up places where people lived, and women and children died because of me.

Sometimes I tell myself that Scheherazade is one of those unseen Iraqi women I massacred. No metaphor intended, I assume the burden of my crime. I can consider myself lucky, Scheherazade would have plenty of good reasons to hate me. But when night falls I get the feeling that she loves me. Go figure: I hate my fat and all day long it torments me. To live with this burden is a torture, my victims haunt me. Yet in this mountain of flesh there is Scheherazade, and after lights out she brings me love. Does she know that I am probably her murderer? That's what I murmured to her in reply to some of her declarations. It doesn't seem to have bothered her. Love is a mystery.

I hate being in Baghdad. But I don't really feel like going back to Baltimore. I haven't told my family that I have put on over two hundred pounds, and I'm terrified at how they might react. No way can I go on a diet. I don't want to lose Scheherazade. If I lost weight it would be like killing her all over again. If my punishment for this war crime is to carry my victim with me as a mound of flesh, then so be it. First of all because justice will have been done, and then because in some inexplicable way it makes me happy. And I'm not being masochistic either, that's not my style.

In the States, back when I was thin, I had quite a few affairs with women. They were generous, no cause for complaint. Sometimes I even fell in love. As everyone knows, the height of earthly happiness is to make love with a woman you love. Well, what I experience with Scheherazade is even better. Is it because she shares my intimacy in the most concrete way? Or is it simply because it's her?

If my existence consisted only of nights, I would be the happiest man on earth. But daytime overwhelms me, in the strictest sense of the term. I have to carry this body around; there's no exaggerating what an ordeal it is to be obese. Even the slaves who built the pyramids did not have burdens as heavy as mine, because I can never put it down even for a moment. The simple joy of walking with a light step, without feeling crushed, is something I really miss. I feel like shouting out and telling normal people to make the most of this unbelievable privilege they don't even seem to be aware of: they can frolic around, carefree, and enjoy the dance of the most ordinary movements. And to think there are people who complain that they have to walk to the store, or that it takes them ten minutes to get to the Metro station!

But the shame is the worst thing of all. What saves me is the fact I'm not the only obese one here. Solidarity with the other fat soldiers keeps me from sinking into despair. I can't imagine any worse suffering than having to put up with the way people stare, or their remarks, or the way they pick on you. I don't know how I used to behave in the old days when I would meet a fatty: did I act like a bastard toward them, too? People always feel smug; they assume that if people are fat they must have been asking for it, you don't get fat for no reason, so come on, boys, we have every right to make them pay, they're not innocent.

It's true, I'm not innocent. Either psychologically or physically. I've committed war crimes, I've been stuffing my face like a monster. But no one is better qualified to judge me than I myself. Our ranks are made up of murderers like me. If they haven't gotten fat, it just goes to show that their misdeeds are not weighing on their conscience. They are worse than I am.

When my buddies and I pork out, the thin soldiers shout at us: "Fuck, guys, stop it! You're disgusting, just watching you eat makes us feel like puking!" We don't say anything, but we talk about it among ourselves: they're the ones, when they've just finished massacring civilians, who go on with life as if nothing has changed, they don't even show any signs of trauma. There are people who stick up for them, saying that they must be suffering from some secret sickness. As if a secret sickness could atone for crimes that are anything but secret! At least we put our guilt right out there on display. Our remorse isn't discreet. Isn't that one way of showing our consideration toward the people we have hurt so badly?

Among ourselves we hate being called fat, so we call each other saboteurs. Our obesity is a wonderful, spectacular act of sabotage. We are costing the Army a lot of money. Our food is cheap, but we eat such terrifying amounts that the bill must be pretty steep. Which is perfect, it's the government's treat. At one point there was this complaint from the Quartermaster Corps, so the bosses decided they would make us pay if we had more than two helpings. Unfortunately for them they didn't test their scheme on a nice guy, but on our buddy Bozo, who is your nasty fat man par excellence. You should have seen Bozo's face when the guard handed him the bill! Bozo made him eat it. Can you believe it! And when he had swallowed it, Bozo shouted, "Consider yourself lucky. If you ever do that again, I'm the one who'll eat you." The issue never came up again.

We cost them a lot in clothes, too: every month we have to change uniforms, because we can't fit in the ones we have anymore. We can't button the pants or the shirt. Apparently the Army had to design a new size: XXXXL. I can't tell you how proud we are. I hope they'll come out with a XXXXXL, because why should we stop when we're on a roll like this. Just between you and me, if they weren't so stupid, they would invent a stretch uniform. I talked about it with the guy in charge of equipment and this is what he said: "No way. The notion of stretch is contrary to the military doctrine. Your clothes have to be stiff, made of non-extensible fabric. Elasticity is our enemy." I thought we were at war with Iraq, and now I find out we're at war with latex.

We cost them a lot in terms of health care. When you're obese, there's always something wrong somewhere. Most of us have heart trouble now: we have to take medication for it. And stuff for high blood pressure. The worst was when they wanted to operate on us. What a screwup. They had this surgeon come from the States, some guy renowned for gastric band surgery: they compress your stomach in a sort of band and you're not hungry anymore. But they don't have the right to insert this thing against your will, and none of us went along with it. We want to be hungry! Food is our drug, our safety valve, we don't want to lose interest in it. You should have seen the surgeon's face when he saw he had no takers. Then the corporals found the weakest link, this guy called Iggy, who visibly had a bigger complex about his weight than we did. They started by getting him all depressed, showing him pictures of what he used to look like: "You were dead handsome, Iggy, when you were thin! What will your girlfriend say when you get back? She won't want anything to do with you!" Iggy broke down, and they operated on him. It worked, he lost weight like crazy. Except that the famous surgeon was pissed he didn't have more success, so he went back to Florida. Not long afterward the gastric band fucked up, it moved, and they had to perform an emergency operation on Iggy. The military surgeons botched it and the poor guy died. Apparently it's inevitable, unless you're a specialist in this operation, there's no way to do it properly. They should have brought the guy back from Florida, but he wouldn't have gotten there in time. In short, Iggy's family filed a lawsuit against the US Army and they won, no problem. The government had to give Iggy's parents a colossal amount of money.

So we are costing them a lot in legal fees, too. Iggy's story gave people ideas. After all, we are all obese because of George W. Bush. I know plenty of guys who will be litigious when they get home. Not me. I'd rather not have anything to do with those folks. They're criminals: in the name of a lie, they sent thousands of innocent people to their death, and they've ruined the lives of the ones who have survived.

I wish I could do them more harm. Unfortunately I belong to a fairly inoffensive species. If anything, eating is still the best way for me to sabotage the system. The problem is the kamikaze nature of my act: I'm not really hitting the target, I'm destroying myself is more like it.

Still, I'm pretty proud of my latest victory: I can't get into a tank anymore. The hatch is too narrow. So much the better, I always hated being in those things, they make you claustrophobic, and you're not as well protected as you think.

Have you seen how long my letter is? I can't get over how much I've written. I needed it. I hope I haven't been force-feeding you.

Sincerely,

Melvin Mapple

A s a rule, I'm not wild about lengthy missives. They are usually the least interesting kind. For over six-teen years I have been getting such a huge amount of mail that I have involuntarily developed an instinctive and experimental theory about the epistolary art. Plus, I have observed that the best letters are never longer than two two-sided letter size pages. (I insist on the two-sided: a love of forests obliges one to be opisthographic. Those who refuse to comply, in the name of some old rule of politeness, have strange priorities.) It's not absurd, it is disrespectful to imagine one has more than that to say, and the lack of courtesy does not make one interesting. Madame de Sévigné put it very well: "Forgive me, I do not have time to be brief." But she's a very poor illustration of my theory: her epistles are always fascinating.

Although he was very different from Madame de Sévigné, Melvin Mapple was offering me yet another incredible exception that confirmed the rule. His letters were so fascinating that they did not even seem long. You could tell they had been written in the grip of absolute necessity: there is no better muse. I could do nothing but reply at once, contrary to my usual habit.

*Paris, March 24, 2009*

Dear Melvin Mapple,

Thank you for your letters, which are more and more interesting. Do not be afraid of force-feeding me: as far as I'm concerned you can never write too much.

Your overeating, and that of your associates, is indeed an act of sabotage. Allow me to congratulate you. You're familiar with the slogan, "Make love, not war." Your slogan should be, "Make fat, not war." That is infinitely praiseworthy. But I am aware of the danger you are in, and I beg you to take care of yourself, to the best of your ability.

Best wishes,

Amélie Nothomb

*Baghdad, March 31, 2009*

Dear Amélie Nothomb,

Your letter came at just the right time. I've been feeling really down. Yesterday we had a run-in with the thin guys in the contingent. It was during dinner. We fat guys are in the habit of eating together: that way we can stuff our faces unashamedly, among ourselves, and we don't need to put up with dirty looks and rude remarks. When one of us outdoes himself by eating more than ever, we congratulate him with this expression we came up with: *"That's the spirit, man!"* It always leaves us in fits of laughter, go figure.

Yesterday evening, probably because there hasn't been much action lately, the other guys came and stood around our table to provoke us.

"Hey, lardasses, what's up?"

Since they started off slowly, we weren't particularly bothered, so we replied with the usual polite formulas.

"How do you manage to eat like that when you're so huge? With all your reserve fat you shouldn't be hungry."

"We have to feed our pounds somehow," said Plumpy.

"I think it's disgusting to see you stuffing your faces like that," said some worthless moron.

"Then don't look at us," I answered.

"Yeah, but how am I supposed to do that? You take up my whole field of vision. We'd love to look at something else but there's always some roll of fat in the way."

We laughed.

"That makes you laugh?"

"Yes. You're funny, so we laugh."

"Maybe it's stealing food from the army that makes you laugh, more like."

"We're not stealing. See, we're eating in plain sight, we're not hiding."

"Yeah sure. That doesn't mean it's not stealing. Every one of you devours ten times our rations."

"We're not stopping you from eating more."

"We don't feel like eating more."

"So where's the problem?"

"You're stealing from the army. So, you're stealing from the United States of America."

"The United States are doing just fine."

"There are loads of people dying of hunger back home."

"That's not our fault."

"How do you know? It's because of thieves and parasites like you that there are poor people at home."

"No. It's because of the thieves a lot higher up."

"So, you admit you're thieves."

"I didn't say that."

Then things started to get out of hand.

Bozo was the first one to get up and hit one of the skinny guys. I tried to stop him. "Can't you see that's what he wants?"

"Then he's gonna get it!"

"Don't! They'll send you to the clink."

"No one can put me there."

"They'll have to widen the door to the clink," shouted the little runt.

At that point I couldn't hold Bozo back anymore. We started fighting. We fat guys had a clear advantage, that was obvious. Our sheer mass would crush anyone. But our Achilles' heel is that if we fall we can't get back up. The other guys had that all figured out. So they went for our ankles, tried to trip us up, or they rolled around on the floor at our feet like bottles. Plumpy fell down, and they rushed over and started beating him. We came to the rescue, and we picked off those wusses who were going at Plumpy as if they were lice. One of the cooks came in with a pot of chili con carne. One guy grabbed the pot from his hands and spilled the boiling chili onto Plumpy's head, laughing, "You hungry? Eat!" The poor guy was screaming. The cook sent for the MPs who came rushing in and pointed their guns at us. That calmed everyone right down. But poor Plumpy has second-degree burns on his face. Bastards.

They took disciplinary action. Not just against the thin guys, either. They held this sort of trial, and no matter how much we protested that we'd been provoked, it wasn't enough to get us off. One guy even said that our size meant we were walking provocateurs, and the official didn't dispute it. We could tell they all agreed.

Bozo and the guy who disfigured Plumpy got the same sentence: three days' detention. He shouted, "So I'm just supposed to stand there and let them insult me?"

"You must not attack your adversary physically."

"Well that's exactly what he was doing!"

"You're playing with words."

What nobody said at the trial, but we all sensed, was how much they hate us. Maybe everyone thinks that plump people are cozy and likable, but if you're obese they despise you, that's just the way it is. Sure, we're not a pleasant sight. I took a closer look at us: the worst thing isn't our bodies, it's our faces. Obesity gives you this hideous expression—blasé, tearful, annoyed, and stupid all at the same time. Not exactly the way to go about it if you want people to like you.

After this parody of justice, we all felt really down. We went for a milkshake in the canteen to try and recover, and the cook who had brought out the chili came over to speak to us. He shared our indignation, he was thinking about Plumpy. For once a thin guy was on our side, so I opened my heart to him. I told them that the reason we ate so much was a kind of rebellion, a violent response to the violence we were being subjected to.

"You don't think it would be smarter to do the opposite?" he suggested.

"What do you mean?" I asked.

"A hunger strike would have more of an impact on public opinion, and everyone would respect you."

We all looked at each other with consternation.

"Have you seen who you're talking to?" I said.

"Anybody can go on a hunger strike," replied this simple soul.

"For a start, I don't think just anybody can. Especially not us. You think we're just some guys with enormous reserves of fat. The truth is that we're the worst junkies on earth. Food, in high doses, is a harder drug than heroin. Porking out is like being sure of your fix, you get these incredible feelings, indescribable thoughts. For guys like us a hunger strike would be like a really heavy-duty form of detox, like those junkies on heroin they have to lock up. No cell is big enough for us. There would be only one way to stop us eating: the straitjacket. But I don't think they make them in our size."

"Gandhi, he—"

"Stop it. What are the odds someone like Bozo could turn into Gandhi? Zero. And my friends and me, the same. To want us to become saints—that's revolting. You're in no danger of becoming one yourself, so what makes you think we can?"

"I don't know, I'm just trying to find a solution for you."

"And as usual, people like you think the only solution can be some form of self-help. Apparently that's all there is for obese people. But you know, obesity is a disease. When someone has cancer, no one has the nerve to suggest they try and help themselves. Yes, I know, you can't compare. It's our fault if we weigh four hundred pounds. We shouldn't have been eating like pigs. Someone who has cancer is a victim, but we're not. We asked for it, we sinned. So we're supposed to redeem ourselves through some saintly act, to atone for what we've done."

"That's not what I meant."

"Well, that's what it amounts to, all the same."

"Shit, guys, I'm on your side."

"I know. That's what's so awful, even our friends don't understand us. Obesity is not a communicable experience."

That made me think of you. Maybe it's an illusion, because of our letter writing: I get the impression that you understand me. I know you suffered from an eating disorder, but of a very different kind. Or maybe it's because you're a writer. People imagine, maybe naively, that novelists have access to a person's soul, to experiences they haven't had themselves. That really got me in Truman Capote's *In Cold Blood*: this impression that the author knew every character intimately, even the minor ones. I would like you to know me that way. It's probably an absurd desire, connected in some way to the scorn people heap upon me, and which makes me suffer. I need a human being who has nothing to do with any of that and who is close to me at the same time: that's what a writer is, right?

You'll tell me that there are other writers and that on top of it English isn't your mother tongue. I know. But you're the one who gave me the idea. I can't help it: you inspire me. In my mind I went through all the living writers. Of course, I'd read an article where you said you answered your letters, which isn't all that common. Still, I swear to you that that's not the reason why. It's as if, with you, everything is possible. It's hard to explain.

Don't worry, I'm not asking you to be my shrink. There's no lack of shrinks around here. I've tried several of them. We talk for three-quarters of an hour in the deepest silence and then they prescribe some Prozac. I refuse to take any of that stuff. I have nothing against shrinks. Except that I'm not sure about the ones from the US Army. What I expect from you is something different.

I want to exist for you. Is that pretentious? I don't know. If it is, forgive me. That's the truest thing I can tell you: I want to exist for you.

Sincerely,

Melvin Mapple

Melvin was hardly the first person who felt he needed to exist for me and that with me everything was possible. Still, rarely had anyone said it to me so simply and clearly.

When someone makes this kind of declaration, I can't really be sure what sort of effect it will have on me: a mixture of emotion and anxiety. If I were to compare this statement to a gift, I would say it's like a dog. The animal itself is touching, but then you think about how you're going to have to look after it, and the fact that you never asked for anything of the kind. On top of it all, the dog is sitting there gazing at you with its kindly eyes, and you say to yourself that it's not its fault, that you can feed it with leftovers, that it will be easy. A tragic mistake, and yet unavoidable.

I'm not comparing Melvin Mapple to a dog, it's this sort of declaration of his that I'm saying is similar to a dog. There are doggie-phrases. It's perfidious.

*Paris, April 6, 2009*

Dear Melvin Mapple,

Your letter was very touching. You do exist for me, rest easy on that score. *In Cold Blood* is a masterpiece. I surely do not possess the power of a Truman Capote, but I do feel as if I know you.

The story about your quarrel and its consequences is terrible and unjust. I think I can understand how you feel. You are being asked to display a greatness of soul, something other people would be incapable of, as if you were trying to apologize for being obese. Tell Plumpy that I've been thinking about him.

I don't know if everything is possible with me, I don't know what that implies. I do know that you exist for me.

Best wishes,

Amélie Nothomb

As I mailed my letter, I reflected that caution had never been my strong point.

*Baghdad, April 11, 2009*

Dear Amélie Nothomb,

Forgive me, I expressed myself poorly in my last letter. You must think it's strange to read that with you everything is possible. I didn't mean it in a disrespectful way. I've never been good at expressing my feelings, and this has already played tricks on me. Thank you for writing that I exist for you, that's very important to me.

Because my life here sucks. If I can exist for you, it makes me feel as if I have another life elsewhere: the life I have in your thoughts. It's not that I want you to imagine me: I don't know what shape your thoughts about me are taking. I'm a figment in your brain: I'm not only what I incarnate in Baghdad. This is a consolation to me.

Your letter was from April 6. The day before, in the

*New York Times,* I read your op-ed piece about President Obama's visit to France: it's odd that they chose you to represent France, when you're actually from Belgium. I was impressed to see your byline in the newspaper. I showed it to my buddies and they said, "Isn't she the one you're writing to?" I was proud. I really liked your article. What you wrote about President Sarkozy was really funny.

On April 7 the British soldiers started to pull out. We didn't meet them. Still, it was really upsetting to see how quickly things were resolved for them. Sure, there are more of us Americans. But what are we doing here? Sometimes I tell myself that if I have gotten so fat in Iraq it's in order to have something to do. It sounds cynical when I write it like this, I know there are things we did in this country: we killed a lot of people, destroyed a lot of their infrastructure, and so on. And I have been a part of all that, it's left me with terrible memories. I'm guilty, I'm not trying to get out of it. And yet it doesn't feel as if it were me. I'm aware, ashamed, I have a mental idea of what it represents, whatever you like, but I don't *feel* anything.

What can give you the feeling of having accomplished something? When I was twenty-five, sleeping rough, I built a kind of shack in a forest in Pennsylvania. It was my achievement, I felt connected to that hut. I feel the same way about my fat. Maybe this fat is my way of leaving a mark on my body, the mark of the evil I've done and cannot feel. It's complicated.

In short, my obesity has become my life's work. I'm still working on it really hard. I eat like a crazy man. Sometimes I tell myself that if I get along with you so well it's because you've never seen me and, above all, because you've never seen me stuffing my face.

When Iggy was alive, he used to say that the reason he'd gotten so fat was to build a barrier between himself and the world. That might have been true for him—the proof is that when his rampart disappeared he died. We all have different theories about our fat. Bozo says that his fat is mean and nasty and that's why he wants to put on as much as possible. I can see what he means. We piss other people off because we inflict the sight of our obesity on them, it's as simple as that. Plumpy thinks his shape has turned him into a baby again. Maybe that's how he feels. No one dares tell him they've never seen such a repulsive baby.

With me it's something else again. When I write that my obesity is my life's work, I'm not joking. That's something you can understand. You have your life's work, it's your literary oeuvre, and it's hard to know what an oeuvre is. We devote our very essence to it and yet it remains a mystery. That's where the comparison stops. Your oeuvre is something worthy of respect, you have every right to be proud of it. But even if there's nothing artistic about mine, it still has significance. Of course I didn't do it on purpose, there's nothing premeditated about it, you could even say I have created it against my will. And yet, from time to time when I'm eating like a pig, I actually feel this sort of enthusiasm which, I suppose, is the enthusiasm of creativity.

When I step on the scales I'm afraid and ashamed because I know that the number I'm about to see, which was already bad enough, will have gotten worse. And yet every time the new verdict appears, every time I cross another unthinkable weight threshold, I'm dismayed, of course, but I'm also impressed: I did this. So there's no limit to my expansion. There's no reason for it to stop.

How high can I go? I say "high" because of the number, but it's not really the right adverb, because I get fat sideways, not upwards. "Far out" might be more appropriate. I'm constantly increasing in volume, as if some inner Big Bang occurred when I arrived in Iraq.

Sometimes after a meal when I sprawl on a chair (they had to order chairs made of reinforced steel) I sit alone with my thoughts for a moment and tell myself, "I must be getting fat at this very instant. My belly must be hard at it." It's fascinating to imagine the transformation of food into all this fat tissue. The body is one hell of a machine. It's too bad I can't feel the moment when the lipids are formed, that would be really interesting.

I already tried to talk about it with the guys, but they said it was obscene. "If getting fat disgusts you so much, then stop," I said. "Don't you start now, too!" they replied. "Of course I won't," I continued, "but since we have no choice in the matter, we could at least feel some joyful curiosity about it. It's an experience, no?" They looked at me as if I were demented.

You understand me better than they do; I know that for you, when you create it's deliberate, and you take a certain pride in it, you go into a mental trance, even if you can read what you've created with the kind of passion that I would find hard to summon when I look at my stomach, I know that you have the constant feeling that your oeuvre has surpassed you. But my oeuvre has surpassed me, too.

When I have the courage to look at myself naked in a mirror, I force myself to go beyond the horror my reflection inspires and I think, "This is me. I am both what I am and what I do. No one else can boast of such an accomplishment. But did I really do this all on my own? How can it be?"

The last I heard, you were working on your sixty-fifth manuscript. Your books aren't long, fair enough. Still, when you look at your sixty-five books you must think, the way I do, that it is simply unbelievable that you produced all that all on your own. Particularly as you aren't done yet, you'll go on writing.

I hope you don't think I'm completely nuts or bad-mannered.

Sincerely,

Melvin Mapple

I confess that I was touched by what he wrote about my op-ed piece in the *New York Times*. "*Vanitas vanitatum sed omnia vanitas.*" As for the rest, even though I did understand what he was trying to say, I felt faintly uncomfortable at the thought that he was likening my ink and paper children to his mound of flesh. Every ounce of pride in me wanted to protest that when I write, it is in a state of asceticism and hunger, I have to reach the depths of my reserves of strength to achieve this supreme act, and putting on weight, even in such daunting proportions, cannot be as trying.

But I could not possibly answer him in such an unfriendly way. I preferred to take his words at face value:

*Paris, April 21, 2009*

Dear Melvin Mapple,

I am now working on my sixty-sixth manuscript and I was struck by how pertinent your comparison is. On reading your letter, I thought about the avant-garde movement in contemporary art known as body art.

I knew a young art student who decided for her dissertation to transform the anorexia she was experiencing at the time into a work of art: she patiently photographed her shrinking body in her bathroom mirror, kept track of how much she lost every day, recorded the figures alongside the clumps of hair she collected, wrote down the date her period stopped, and so on. Her dissertation, which needed no commentary, was presented in the form of a syllabus entitled "My Anorexia," and it contained only photographs, dates, a weight log, and clumps of hair, right until the end which in her case, was not death, but page 100, since that was the maximum number of pages allowed. She had barely enough strength to defend her dissertation before her professors, who gave her the highest mark. Then she was admitted to a clinic. At present she is doing much better and I would not rule out the possibility that her academic endeavor had a great deal to do with it. Anorexics need to know that their suffering is acknowledged, not condemned. The young woman had found a very ingenious way to do this while resolving the ever thorny problem of the dissertation.

*Mutatis mutandis*, you could follow her example. I don't know if you've been photographing your weight gain, but it's not too late to start. Keep a record of the figures and all the physical and mental symptoms, how it evolves. You must surely have some photographs from the days when you were thin, which you could use for the beginning of your notebook. You will go on putting on weight, so you can take ever more impressive photographs. Make sure you emphasize those parts of your body your corpulence seems to favor. But don't neglect the underprivileged areas for all that, such as your feet, which may not have swollen as much as your belly or your arms, but your shoe size must have gone up all the same.

You see, Melvin, you were right: your obesity is your oeuvre. You are surfing a wave of artistic modernity. You must do something about it right away because the thing that is fascinating about what you're doing is not just the result, it's also the process. To make sure the big shots of the body art world recognize you as one of their own, perhaps you should also keep a record of everything you eat. In the case of the young anorexic girl, that was a far simpler chapter: every day, nothing. In your case, it may well prove tedious. Don't lose heart. Think of your work, which, as an artist, is your sole raison d'être.

Best wishes,

Amélie Nothomb

At the time I mailed this letter I could not say what my precise state of mind was. I would have been incapable of saying exactly how much of my letter was cordial sincerity and how much was irony. Melvin Mapple had earned my respect and sympathy, but I had the same problem with him that I have with one hundred percent of the other creatures on earth, human or otherwise: the barrier. You meet someone, in person or in writing. The first stage consists in acknowledging that the other person exists: at times this is a moment of wonder. In that instant you are like Robinson Crusoe and Friday on the beach on the island, you gaze at each other, stupefied, delighted that there can be another person in this world who is both other and close to you at the same time. Your existence seems all the more intense in the knowledge that the other person is aware of it, and you feel a wave of enthusiasm for this providential individual who is there to respond to you. You attribute a fabulous name to this creature: friend, lover, comrade, host, colleague— depending. It is an idyll. The alternation between identity and otherness ("That's just like me! That's just the opposite of me!") leaves you in a daze, a childlike rapture. You are so intoxicated that you cannot see the danger that lies just ahead.

And suddenly, the other is there, behind the door. You sober up all at once, you don't know how to tell him that he wasn't invited. It's not that you don't like him anymore, it's that you like him when he is other, that is, someone who is not you. And now this other is trying to get closer, as if he wanted to assimilate you or be assimilated by you.

You know you are going to have to spell things out. There are various ways to go about this, explicitly or implicitly. Whatever the case, it is a rough passage. Over two-thirds of relationships fail to make it. Instead there is hostility, misunderstanding, silence, sometimes hatred. Bad faith presides over these failures, alleging that if the friendship had been sincere, there would have been no problem. That's not true. This crisis is inevitable. Even if you genuinely adore the other person, you're not prepared to have them move in with you.

It would be an illusion to believe that an epistolary exchange could protect you from such a pitfall. It cannot. Other people can move in and impose themselves in so many ways. I've lost count of how many correspondents have eventually told me that they were just like me, that they were writers just like me. Melvin Mapple had found a very particular manner of assimilating himself to me.

People are like countries. It's wonderful that there are so many of them, and that a perpetual continental drift allows you to meet all these new islands. But if the plate tectonics leave the unknown territory against your shore, hostility instantly arises. There are only two solutions: war or diplomacy.

I tend to favor the latter. However, I did not know whether my last letter to Melvin had been diplomatic or not; my need to send it had prevailed. His reaction would inform me as to the nature of my message.

*Diplomatic letter* is a pleonasm. The etymology of "diplomat" is the ancient Greek word *diploma*, "paper folded in two," in other words, a letter. Diplomacy began with correspondence. A letter can indeed be a way of saying things pleasantly. Whence a historical contamination of both practices: a diplomat often writes a great number of missives, and the epistolary genre often adopts diplomatic mannerisms.

More than any other form of writing, a letter is addressed to a reader. I began to wait for my reader's response with diffuse anxiety. Oddly enough, it wasn't impatience. The absence of a letter would have been the appropriate reaction.

Tired of my life in France, I went to Belgium to rest for a week. For seven days I enjoyed an unbelievable luxury: epistolary absolute zero. Correspondence is no different from anything else: an excess is as unbearable as a shortage. I've had more than my fair share of both extremes. I think I still prefer excess, but the fact remains that it's very trying. A shortage of mail, which was my fate during my long adolescence, makes you feel like you've been given the cold shoulder, you've been rejected, you are plague-stricken. Excess propels you into a pond full of piranhas who are all trying to take a big bite out of you. The happy medium, which must be very pleasant, is *terra incognita* to me.

The only solution I could find to this deadlock was to flee. The upside of this situation is that you experience happiness of a sort with which very few people are acquainted: the joy of receiving no epistles, the headiness of not having to write any.

It is a very particular form of exultation, where a demonic little voice never stops murmuring in your head, "You are not in the process of opening an envelope that weighs a ton, you are not in the process of writing out the words 'Dear Thingummy,' you are not catching up on your correspondence . . . " This refrain of internal whispering multiplies your pleasure fifteen-fold.

But all good things come to an end. On April 29 I took the train back to Paris and on April 30 I was back at my desk. It was covered with a pile of envelopes of varying sizes.

I took a deep breath and sat down. To confront the enemy I have a method: I begin by sorting. I separate the unknown senders from the known ones, then further sort the ones I'm looking forward to reading into a pile on the left, and the ones that look like they might be tedious on the right. As always, this latter group is boundless. It is a law of nature, even if I repeat myself: the desired letter is short, the undesirable one is voluminous. This is true for every level of desire: a refined dish will not spill over the plate, vintage wines are served parsimoniously, exquisite creatures are slender, and a tête-à-tête is the encounter you anticipate most eagerly.

This rule is so deep-rooted that it is pointless trying to influence it. How many times have I suggested to those correspondents of mine who are likable enough but seriously verbose not to send me more than one two-sided page? How many times have I explained to them that this is how they will appear in their best light?

After two or three letters where, very kindly, they do honor my wish, there come the inexorable additions: a simple postcard to start with, then an extra page, and finally the same old sandwich-letters that turn an envelope into a hopeless picnic wrapper. Format, like clothes, makes the man; it would seem it can't be helped.

Nor is there anything I can do, as long as my preference lies the way of simple letters rather than epistolary *choucroute garnie*. So I begin with these ones, skimming through the contents to determine whether I can read them without vomiting. I save the letters deserving of the name for last—the brief missives, in other words. It is the policy of dessert.

That April 30, as I was doing my sorting, I recognized an envelope from Iraq. It's not that I had forgotten about Melvin Mapple, but for one week he had no longer been front and center in my mind. I felt the mixture of joy and despondency which he now aroused in me. Faithful to my technique, I began by opening all the envelopes with a pair of scissors. It took me an hour. I read the American soldier's letter first of all:

*Baghdad, April 26, 2009*

Dear Amélie Nothomb,

Thank you for your letter, which filled me with enthusiasm. You've done more than just understand me, you've given me a brilliant idea. What a pity I didn't write to you as soon as I got to Baghdad! I would have been taking pictures of my weight gain right from the start, and my obesity notebook would have been even more spectacular. But you're right, it's never too late, and I have a few photos of the days when I weighed a hundred and twenty pounds, then a hundred and eighty, so it will give an impression of progression all the same. Thanks to you, now when I weigh myself in the morning I am filled with joy: not a day goes by where I haven't put on weight. Of course there are good days and bad days: sometimes I only put on a quarter of a pound, but other times I gain two whole pounds in twenty-four hours and that is truly gratifying.

There was no need for you to feel awkward suggesting I keep track of everything I eat. Now I go to dinner with my notebook and you cannot imagine how much fun it is writing everything down. My buddies are in on the project and they help me, which is pretty useful, because you always forget some little thing like peanuts or a bag of chips. This artistic project is *our* project, and I'm not just my own work of art, I'm also my buddies' work of art. They encourage me to eat, they take my picture. I was dreading they might steal the idea and start their own notebooks devoted to their obesity, but I was wrong, they're not the least bit tempted. They don't have any aesthetic sense, but they're prepared to support mine. My nickname is Body Art. I love it.

I didn't hide the fact that it was your idea, and they were impressed. Who else but you could have come up with such an idea? Not only did it have to be a writer, it had to be *this* writer. You know, I've read a lot in my life, and I've gotten to know, so to speak, quite a few authors, by reading their complete works, and I can assure you: this is definitely an Amélie Nothomb sort of idea.

I really appreciate it. Thanks to your last letter, you've helped me find a meaning in life. It seems to me that ought to be the goal of every writer. You deserve to practice this fine profession. When I told you that my obesity was my life's work, I thought you were going to make fun of me. Well, not only did you not make fun of me, you gave me the means to fulfill my dream and share it with others.

Without the notebook you advised me to keep, how could I have explained to other people what I was doing?

It's all the more important, given the fact that my art has a political significance. My obesity is anything but gratuitous, because it has carved my commitment into my body: to make the entire world see the unprecedented horror of this war. Obesity has become eloquent: my own expanse reflects the scale of human destruction on either side. It also speaks of how unlikely it would be for me to return to a semblance of normality: just suppose it were even possible to lose over two hundred pounds, it would take ages, and untold effort. And how does a guy like me look after he's melted away? His skin will be flaccid and hanging like an old man's. Not to mention the inevitable relapses, because you can never recover from such a serious addiction.

Every modern war leaves indelible marks wherever it goes; of all the lasting damage caused by the war in Iraq, obesity, I think, will be the most emblematic. Human fat will be for George W. Bush what napalm was for Johnson.

It's not that justice will be done. But at least the accusation will be heard. There's no better way than through a work of art. When we get home it will be easy for me and my buddies to get the attention of the media and, who knows, maybe even some gallery owners. So it's important not to lose weight. Which is just as well, because we have no intention of losing any.

Sincerely,

Melvin Mapple

This letter plunged me into deep dismay. I was embarrassed by the opening: I always feel uneasy when someone praises me or thanks me effusively if I haven't deserved it. And while, to be sure, I hadn't intended to be cynical in my previous letter, I recalled that it was ironical all the same. Plainly, the soldier had failed to grasp this. I squirmed.

It got worse after that. The thing is, he truly believed in his artistic project. All I had done was tell him what the anorexic young woman had accomplished: it was a true story, but it was nothing more than a final dissertation. Melvin Mapple, however, never seemed to doubt for one moment his status as a work of art, and what was worse, its imminent success. "It will be easy for me and my buddies to get the attention of the media"—I felt like asking him what made him so sure—"and, who knows, maybe even some gallery owners"—my poor Melvin, what sort of world was he living in?! My heart sank at the sight of his unwavering optimism, so typical of those who just do not know.

And finally, the last straw: his resolution not to lose weight. I was providing that gang of obese soldiers with the pretext they needed to wall themselves up in their fat. They would die from it. And it would be my fault.

I reread the letter. Mapple was out of his mind. "Human fat will be for George W. Bush what napalm was for Johnson": it was blatantly obvious that such a comparison was both inappropriate and indecent. The soldiers and their fat were a matter for the Americans only, and would disappear with them, whereas napalm had been dumped upon an occupied country and would go on for a long time poisoning the existence of the civilian population.

Melvin might call himself an artist, but I had not known how to provide him with one essential artistic quality: doubt. An artist who does not doubt is as obnoxious as the lady's man who instantly assumes he's in occupied territory. Behind every work of art lies the enormous pretension of exhibiting one's vision of the world. If such obvious arrogance is not counterbalanced by the tribulations of doubt, all that remains is a monster who is to art what a fanatic is to faith.

It must be said in my defense that although the Mapple case might defy comparison, it was not unusual for people to send me samples of their work: a page of writing, a drawing, a CD. When I had the time, I would reply and tell them very simply what I thought. You can always find a way to be sincere without being disagreeable. But this was his own body that Melvin had submitted to me. How could I find the necessary detachment to express myself on the subject?

I was not refuting the essence of what I had written to him. No, the rub was that now the soldier was expecting his art to receive public recognition.

I decided to be pragmatic and downplay the situation. After all, Melvin Mapple was not the first aspiring artist to come face-to-face with the harsh reality of the art market.

If he felt like trying his luck, who was I to dissuade him? There was no reason I should take his future disappointment so much to heart. Given the present state of affairs, he would be in Baghdad for a long while still, and he would surely not be crazy enough to go trying his luck with Iraqi gallery owners. And there would be plenty of time to worry about his project once he was back in the States, assuming he didn't give up on it in the meantime. Feeling somewhat calmer, I wrote:

*Paris, April 30, 2009*

Dear Melvin Mapple,

I am glad to see how enthusiastic you are. But do take care of yourself. It's been a while since you mentioned Scheherazade. How is she? This will be a short letter, I'm behind with my correspondence.

Best wishes,

Amélie Nothomb

I mailed this letter feeling satisfied that I had found the right tone, and the ideal distance between coolness and fervor. If the soldier no longer had any doubts, it was because he was so inclined by nature: it would be absurd of me to incriminate myself, and typical of my own tendency to make myself feel guilty for all the woes in the universe.

There's no better way to get a new perspective on things than to read a stranger's letter: an actress from Saint-Germain-des-Prés wrote to me on April 23; I'd never heard of her before. She said she had seen me at the Odéon Métro station on April 15, in tears. This had upset her greatly, but she hadn't dared come and speak to me. It was the first time she had ever seen me, and this was just how she imagined me. She felt very close to me and now she asked if I would write a text for her that she could perform on stage, something which would help me transcend my suffering. She sent several photographs of herself to back up her request.

I immersed myself in her photographs, wondering all the while what I could have been crying about at the Odéon Métro station on April 15: what could have gotten into me, to go there to cry my eyes out? I probed my memory in search of a cause for such mid-April despair, when suddenly it became perfectly obvious: the crying woman she had seen in the Métro was not me. The actress had seen a likeness between me and another strange woman sobbing at the Odéon. For her own dark reasons that was how she pictured me. My latent flea-market-psychoanalyst self posited that it was her own tearful face in the reflection of the window of a train passing through the Odéon station that this woman from Saint-Germain-des-Prés had seen, in fact, and unable to recognize her own identity she had attributed it to an ectoplasm whom she had christened Amélie Nothomb.

Why me? Who could say. I am about to write something grave and true: I am that porous creature upon whom people call to play a devastating role in their lives. We all have our narcissistic side, and it would be only too easy to blame these recurrent phenomena on whatever it is in me that is exceptional, but nothing in me is more exceptional than this unfortunate porosity of mine, which I suspect of wreaking havoc. People sense that I am fertile soil for their secret vegetable patch: Melvin Mapple had found what he needed in my loam to nourish his artistic fantasies; the actress wept her lettuce leaves in my garden of sprouting tears; it is incredible how often the masses toss the contents of their seed packets in the direction of my private preserve. I find it moving, but I cannot rejoice, because I know I shall be held responsible should any of these personal projects fail, projects about which I know nothing.

I would reply to the actress in a month or so, which is my usual time frame and which I would have done better to respect in Melvin Mapple's case. So many letters, it was endless. Don't get me wrong: I love it. I love reading letters and writing them, especially with certain people. However, from time to time I need to clean out my system, the better to enjoy the activity.

What are you supposed to do when there are forty or more epistles requiring your attention? You sort. For example, I refused to read the thirty-five homework assignments sent to me by a French teacher who was counting on me to correct her week's workload. "My students have read your books, so you owe them," she wrote, seeming to think that her absurd reasoning actually meant something.

That afternoon I drank a Grimbergen while taking deep delight in the substance of the numerous letters I had saved until last. I was enjoying the pleasure of having regained my appetite. Epistolary hunger is an art, and I aim to excel in it.

The next day several planetary events occurred that went unreported by the newspapers. They were all busy talking about a pandemic, and I suppose they were right—the press is good at choosing its actions but not its subjects—for there was indeed an epidemic raging, but it was an epidemic of great and beautiful risks, of success.

Life continued its Parisian amble. There arose a sudden and unexpected interest in a book published during the reign of Louis XIV: an absolute gem of refinement, despite the era, which was one of absolute power. The book tells a story that was meant to have taken place one hundred and twenty years earlier. No one, anymore, is even aware of this huge gap between the two eras. Such a dizzying, scarcely perceptible artifice is the hallmark of a masterpiece. The Chinese who live in France are no more foreign than I am. I will never stop rhapsodizing over this country, which is more than ever the country of *La Princesse de Clèves.*

I worked out that Melvin Mapple would receive my letter on May 4. I did not dwell on it. This is how you must go about it. If you follow the path of a letter in your mind, one way or another it will not reach its destination. You must let the recipient do his work. Experience has shown that letters are never read the way one imagines: therefore, it is preferable not to imagine anything.

I have been a letter writer for far longer than I have been a writer, and I probably would not have become a writer—at least, not this writer—had I not started off as an assiduous letter writer. Already at the age of six I was forced by my parents to write one letter a week to my maternal grandfather, a stranger who lived in Belgium. My brother and my older sisters were subjected to the same regime. Each of us had to fill an entire letter-sized page addressed to this gentleman. He answered with one page per child. "Tell him what happened at school," my mother would suggest. "He won't be interested," I retorted. "That depends on how you tell it," she explained.

It used to bore me stiff. It was a worse nightmare than homework. I had to fill the blank paper with sentences that might, at a push, interest my faraway ancestor. That is the only period in my life when I have experienced the anxiety of the empty page, but it lasted for years, all through my childhood—for centuries, in other words.

"Comment on what he's written to you," my mother advised one day, on seeing me draw a blank. Commenting means describing the other person's words. Upon reflection, that was what my grandfather had been doing: his letters commented on mine. Not a bad idea. So I did likewise. My missives commented on his commentary. And so on. It was a bizarre, dizzying dialogue but not devoid of interest. The nature of the epistolary genre was revealed to me: a form of writing devoted to another person. Novels, poems, and so on, were texts into which others were free to enter, or not. Letters, on the other hand, did not exist without the other person, and their very mission, their significance, was the epiphany of the recipient.

Just as it is not enough to write a book to be a writer, it is not enough to write a letter to be a letter writer. Very often I receive missives in which the sender has forgotten or never knew that he or she might be addressing me, or someone else. These are not letters. Or sometimes I might write a letter to someone, and that person might send me an answer that is not an answer; not that I asked him a question, but there is nothing in his text that gives me any indication that he has even read my letter. That, to me, is not a letter. To be sure, it is not given to everyone to have a talent for repartee; nevertheless, it is something that can be learned and which would be beneficial to a great many people.

Dear Amélie Nothomb,

Thank you for your encouraging words on April 30. Scheherazade is fine, don't worry. If I haven't mentioned her, that's because nothing has changed on that end. We've had news from some soldiers who went home two months ago. Alarming news. Far from diminishing, the physical and psychological ailments they were suffering from here have gotten worse. The doctors looking after them talk about their reinsertion: the same word they'd use if we were getting out of prison. And apparently ex-prisoners do a better job at reinserting themselves. A prisoner is less of a stranger than one of us.

No one is crazy enough to want to come back to Iraq, but the guys say they have no life left in the US. The sad thing is they have nowhere else to go. And anyway, the problem is not the place. They say they don't know what to make of their lives anymore, what to live for. Six years of war have erased everything that came before. I know what they mean.

I think I told you, more than once, that I wanted to go back to the States. Now I realize I wrote that as if it went without saying, but I'd never really thought it through.

What will I find at home? Nothing and nobody, other than the army. My parents are ashamed of me. I've lost all trace of the people who used to be my friends, even supposing that shared misery constitutes friendship worthy of the name. And let's not forget the detail of my weight. Do you really want to see people again when you've put on three hundred pounds? Three hundred pounds! If I weighed three hundred pounds, already that would be obese. Well I don't weigh three hundred pounds, I've filled out by three hundred pounds! It's as if I were three people.

I've started a family. Scheherazade and I have a child. It would all be perfectly charming if the family didn't consist solely of me. Hey guys, let me introduce my wife and kid, they're in here keeping nice and warm, that's why you can't get a good look at them, I prefer to keep them inside, it's more intimate, it's easier too, to protect them and feed them, what's so surprising about that, there are women who breast-feed their children, I've decided to feed my family from the inside.

In short, for the first time, I am beginning to realize that I don't feel like going home. I hate being here, but at least there is a framework to my life and my human relations. Above all, here in Iraq, people know who I am. I don't want to see the expression on my parents' faces when they see me again for the first time, I don't want to hear what they're going to say.

Once again, what is saving me is my artistic project. I can never thank you enough for that. It's the only dignity I have left. Do you think my father and mother will understand? Right, maybe I shouldn't ask myself that question. You don't become an artist so that your parents will understand you. Still, I do think about it.

I'm afraid they'll make fun of me. If I had an agent, or someone like that, I wouldn't feel so ridiculous. You were in the States not long ago, maybe you met some people there who could help me? Or maybe you know of an art gallery in New York or Philadelphia? Or someone influential at the *New York Times*? I'm sorry to bother you with this. I don't know who else to ask.

Sincerely,

Melvin Mapple

I raised my eyes to the sky. This soldier was only the 2,500th person to imagine that I belong to a network of public relations on a global scale and in every domain. So many people view me as the providential person who will be able to get them into the most sophisticated circles or introduce them to inaccessible individuals. One day a Belgian nun wrote to me saying she wanted to meet Brigitte Bardot: not only did her request seem perfectly natural to her, but in the eyes of this nun it went without saying that I was the person to contact in order to fulfill her dream. (I've gotten letters from people begging me to put in a word for them with Amélie Mauresmo, Sharon Stone, and Jean-Michel Jarre. Go figure.)

It is incredibly irritating, people use me as an address book; I am amazed by the fact that they constantly solicit me for favors. I would never, personally, dare make such a request of anyone; I wouldn't even think of it. What incredible bad taste, to take something as good-natured as the correspondence between writer and reader and confuse it with cronyism or an employment agency.

I had been fond of Melvin Mapple, I thought he was different. I was dismayed to see him displaying such com-

mon behavior. At least he did apologize for bothering me
with it. It was a nice change from such horrifying declarations as "I thought you might have fun helping me," or the
equally genuine "If you help me in my endeavors it might
give meaning to your life."

Once I got over my mood, I became aware of just how
worrying this letter really was. The soldier was informing
me that if his status as an artist was not recognized he
would refuse to go back to the United States. Did he have
any right to do this? Fortunately, it seemed that he did not.
Moreover, at what point would he be able to consider himself a recognized artist? I have noticed that the criteria for
recognition vary dramatically from one individual to the
next. Some people will think they are recognized artists if
their next-door neighbor tells them so; there are others for
whom no recognition is valid short of the Nobel Prize. I
was hoping that Melvin Mapple would belong to the first
category.

So although I had initially thought I would turn down
his request, I suddenly saw the situation in a more amus-
ing light. I didn't know anyone in artistic circles in the
United States. In Europe I did know a few gallery owners,
in Paris and Brussels. It would be difficult to get any
Parisians to go along with such a bizarre enterprise, as it
would be with the majority of their colleagues in Brussels,
but I did know of one vague sort of gallery (more of a *bar
à bière* than a gallery, to be honest) in the Marolles quartier,
where the owner, a man by the name of Cullus, was a friend
of mine. I immediately called and told him how he could
contribute to a worthy cause: an American soldier in
Baghdad had gone on the opposite of a hunger strike, let's
call it a satiety strike, to protest against the invasion of

Iraq, and he viewed his obesity as a sort of militant body art. All he needed to obtain recognition was the approval of an art gallery somewhere on the planet. A pure formality, because it went without saying, alas, that the soldier could not exhibit himself in all his opulence in Brussels. He needed the name of a gallery just to add to his file, the way a writer needs the name of a publisher to feel she exists. Cullus embraced my suggestion enthusiastically, and asked me to spell out the soldier's name for him so that he could add it to his catalog. I did as he requested, suppressing a desire to laugh, because the catalog in question was a slate where the beers were listed on the left and the artists on the right. Cullus asked me to send him a photograph of Mapple for his portfolio, and we said goodbye.

Delighted, I wrote to the American:

*Paris, May 9, 2009*

Dear Melvin Mapple,

I don't know any gallery owners in your country, but I do know a few in mine. I have excellent news: the renowned Cullus Gallery in Brussels will be delighted to include you in their catalog. I imagine it won't be possible for you to go there, even though Cullus would surely be only too happy to meet you and exhibit you. That doesn't matter: what does, is that you can now affirm that you have a gallery, which gives you official status as an artist. Isn't that wonderful? You will be able to go back to the United States with your head held high, and you needn't be ashamed of your obesity—you can even be proud of it, since it is your work of art and has been recognized as such.

I think I can understand how difficult, even impossible, it will be for you to go back to the US. But this is a problem that concerns your friends now more than it does you yourself. I cannot promise you that you are going to be living in a fairytale. But at least you will have a purpose in life, something that is so sorely lacking among the soldiers you wrote to me about. Bravo!

Best wishes,

Amélie Nothomb

This episode put me in a good mood. I would like to point out that there was not the shadow of a cynical or even ironical intent in what I had done. Cullus in the Marolles may not have been Perrotin in the Marais, but he was nevertheless a gallery owner worthy of the name. I had qualified his gallery as renowned because it did indeed have a certain notoriety in Brussels. And I did not think there was anything dishonorable about the fact that they sold beer first and foremost: there are more beer drinkers than there are collectors of contemporary art, that's just the way it goes. As for me, when I go to see Cullus, it is for his *bière blanche*, but while I'm savoring it, I take the opportunity to look at the exhibition, and I gaze at the works and enjoy them all the more intensely for the pleasure I take in my beer.

I know that all the other art galleries thought Cullus was some sort of joker who had nothing to do with their cabal. That is not my opinion, nor would it have been the opinion of Melvin Mapple, I am sure. So my satisfaction was that of someone who has introduced two people who were destined to meet.

Suddenly I realized that I had forgotten one detail.

Relieved that I had not yet closed the envelope, I added this postscript:

Cullus the gallery owner would like a photograph of you as you are now. Send it to me and I will pass it on.

This was Saturday, so I rushed to mail the letter before the last noontime collection.

The following week, I had a visit from a Hungarian student who was devoting his thesis to me at the University of Budapest; he spoke very strange French, which gave me the pleasant impression that I was a Voivode or an archimandrite. Eastern European countries do wonders for your ego, I've often noticed.

I met a talented young novelist I'd been wanting to get to know for years. Unfortunately she was so doped on Xanax that communication was scrambled. Even though she was sitting right across from me, I felt like my words had to transit several worlds to reach her brain. Eventually she explained:

"I can't seem to cut down on my dose of tranquilizers."

"Isn't it dangerous?" I asked, aware that my question was perfectly stupid.

"Of course it is. I can't do without them. How do you manage to withstand the pressure?"

"I don't know."

"Don't you think it's a terrible stress to be a novelist?"

"I do. I'm terribly stressed."

"So why aren't you taking tranquilizers? You think it's necessary to suffer, is that it?"

"No."

"Why do you accept your suffering, then?"

"I suppose I don't want to damage my brain."

"So you think I'm damaging mine?"

"I have no idea."

"Don't you think that suffering causes greater harm to your brain?"

"Let's not exaggerate. Writing can be extremely pleasurable, for a start. What makes me suffer is all the anxiety that comes with it."

"Whence the need for tranquilizers."

"I'm not so sure. Without anxiety, there can be no pleasure."

"Of course there can. Try pleasure without anxiety."

"Are you under contract to the pharmaceutical industry?"

"Yeah, really. Go on being anxious, if you enjoy it so much. I see you haven't answered my question. How do you deal with the stress?"

"Badly."

"That's more like it."

She was funny. Even though I liked her well enough, I realized I would have preferred a letter from her to her physical presence. Could this be a pathological attitude, due to the hegemony of letters in my life? There are very few individuals whose company is more pleasant than a letter from them would be—assuming, naturally, that they possess a minimum of epistolary talent. Most people would consider such a realization to be a confession of weakness, a lack of energy, an inability to confront reality. I've been told on occasion, "You don't like people in real life." I object: why should someone be more real just because you have him or her across from you? Why shouldn't their truth stand out better, or simply differently, in a letter?

The only thing I know for certain is that it depends on the individual. There are some people who improve on personal acquaintance, and others who improve on being read. In any event, even when I like someone to the point of living with him, I have to have him write to me, too: no connection seems complete unless it includes an element of correspondence.

Some people I know solely through an epistolary connection. Naturally I would be curious to see them in person, but that is in no way indispensable. And to meet them would not necessarily be without consequence. In this respect, correspondence raises that important literary question: should we meet writers?

There is no answer to this, because there are too many answers. Indisputably, some authors do their work great harm. I have spoken with people who met Montherlant, and they were sorry they had done so: one man told me that pursuant to a brief conversation with that writer, he had been so disgusted by the man that he never read another line of the work he had once so admired. Conversely, I have been told that Giono's prose was even more beautiful if one had had the good fortune to meet him. And then there are those authors you would never have dreamt of reading had you not met them, not to mention the most numerous category of all, those who in real life leave us every bit as indifferent as their books have done.

Similarly, there can be no law governing correspondents. But my natural tendency advises me not to meet them, not so much out of caution, as for the reason so sublimely expressed in a preface by Proust: reading enables us to discover the other, while preserving the depths one has solely when alone.

And I found, indeed, that the young novelist would have done better to get to know me in my more interesting condition of solitude. The opposite would no doubt have been true as well: her pharmaceutical proselytism had traumatized me to no small degree.

By the time the next letter from the American arrived, I had forgotten that I had asked him for a photograph. It hit me right in the face: a naked, hairless thing, so enormous that it spilled over the edge. A blister in full expansion: you could sense the flesh constantly searching for new opportunities to spread and swell, to conquer new terrain. The fresh flab must have to cross continents of fatty tissue to blossom on the surface, before crusting over like bacon draped over a roast to become the support for even newer fat. Thus is the void conquered by obesity: to add weight, the body annexes the empty space.

The sex of this tumor could not be determined. While the individual stood facing the camera lens, the sheer abundance of rolls of fat hid the genitals. Gigantic breasts would seem to imply that this was a woman, but drowned as they were among so many other folds and protuberances, they lost their full teat-like impact, resembling nothing so much as rubber tires.

It took me a moment to recall that all this efflorescence was human, and that it was indeed my correspondent, Private Melvin Mapple. I have had more than my share of the always astonishing experience that consists in putting a face to a person's handwriting: in the soldier's case, it would be difficult to isolate from the body a face so polderized by fat. He had already lost his neck, because the isthmus that was supposed to connect the head to the torso did not display the trait of relative narrowness which enables one to identify that segment of the body. I thought how it would be impossible to guillotine this man, or even oblige him to wear a necktie.

As I looked at Melvin Mapple I could see he still had features, but you could no longer qualify them: you could not say whether his nose was hooked or turned up, his mouth was large or small, his eyes were this way or that; you could say he had a nose, a mouth, and a pair of eyes, and that was already something, for you could not say as much for his chin, which had disappeared long before. It gave you the anxious feeling that a time would come when even these basic elements would also sink deeper and deeper until they were no longer visible. And it made you wonder how, when that day came, would this living creature manage to breathe, to speak, to see.

His eyes were like the recessed tucks in a padded armchair. And while the eyes are supposed to be the mirror of the soul, there was nothing one could read in Melvin Mapple's eyes beyond their effort to force their way through to the outside world. His nose was a curl of cartilage in an ocean of flesh, his nostrils a precarious treasure: one day this power socket would be covered over by the masonry of his fat. One could only hope that the man would still be able to breathe through his mouth; no doubt it would hold out until the bitter end, driven by the instinct for survival which every assassin shares.

It was indeed hard to look at what remained of his mouth and not be reminded that it was to blame, this minuscule orifice that had opened the gates to the invaders.

We all know that the brain is in charge and yet, when we meet a sculptor, we observe his hands; when we spent time with a perfumer, we steal glances at his nose; a ballerina's legs are more entrancing than her head is. Melvin Mapple's lips had well and truly been the pioneers of this suffocating expansion into space, and his teeth had voluntarily undertaken to chew all that food. His mouth exerted a fascination not unlike that of History's great murderers.

I had come to know this man through our correspondence. At the end of his hypertrophied arms his fingers seemed microscopic, and I could only surmise how difficult it must be to write with such a volume of fat. To reach me, his writing had to transit so much flesh. The distance between Iraq and France seemed far less daunting than that which separated the soldier's brain from his hand.

Melvin Mapple's brain: how could one help but think of it? Gray matter is made up essentially of fat; in the case of excessive weight loss, the brain suffers aftereffects. What happens in the opposite case? Does the brain get bigger, or does it simply acquire more fat? If so, what effect would that have on thought? The intelligence of a Churchill or a Hitchcock had not suffered on account of its owner's obesity, that much is clear, but beyond a doubt, when you find yourself dragging that much weight around it must influence your thinking in one way or another.

Never had I taken so long to start reading what he had written:

*Baghdad, May 14, 2009*

Dear Amélie Nothomb,

Thank you for the wonderful news! I am overjoyed that

the famous Cullus Gallery in Brussels is including me in their catalog, and I know how much I owe you for your contribution. I've already told everyone here about it: it's a major event. I've enclosed the photograph you asked for.

Now I feel like an established artist. And as such I don't feel the least bit embarrassed showing you my photograph. Otherwise I would have been too ashamed for you to find out what I look like. Now I tell myself that it is art, so I'm proud.

I hope the photograph is appropriate; it was taken two weeks ago. Please tell the Belgian gallery owner how grateful I am. Thanks again.

Sincerely,

Melvin Mapple

This was a very American attitude: everything was fine provided it was official and aboveboard. If you came out and proclaimed the phenomenon, you eliminated any risk of embarrassment. And while I might appreciate the fact that Melvin had no complexes, I did nevertheless feel somewhat uncomfortable with the way he flaunted himself—while reproaching myself for my European prudishness. He was happy, after all: that was all that mattered.

Still, I could not help but place the image and the writing side by side: the photograph in my left hand, the letter in my right. My eyes went from one to the other as if I were trying to persuade myself that the human message had actually come from this pudding, and that all the touching missives I'd received over the few last months had come from this ton. I was so perplexed by the thought that I blushed. To cut things short I slipped the print into an envelope, wrote Cullus's address on the outside and added a note explaining that this was the new artist we had talked about.

I did not answer the American right away. I let myself believe that I was waiting for a reaction from the gallery owner. To be honest, I had been intimidated by my confrontation with the obese amoeba. I just did not feel up to resuming the civilized tone of our correspondence right away: "Thank you, dear Melvin, for the charming photograph . . . "—no, courtesy had its limits. I was somewhat annoyed with myself for being so impressionable, but there was nothing I could do about it.

As I never lacked a backlog of letters, I set about writing to people of ordinary corpulence. To erase the very memory of the photograph, I filled out my tax return: I have often found that soul-destroying tasks help one to live.

That day I also received a letter from P. asking me for a preface. Not one day goes by without at least one letter of this kind. I systematically refuse, for that very reason. The fact remains that people would make my existence so much easier if they would spare me these constant entreaties—when it's not a preface, it's their manuscript that wants reading, or I must teach them how to write.

The fact that I reply to the letters I receive has given rise to considerable confusion, to erroneous and contradictory interpretations. The first of these is that my letter writing is some sort of savvy marketing ploy on my part. Yet the figures are eloquent: I have hundreds of thousands of readers, and although I write letters like a maniac, I've never had more than two thousand correspondents, which is already sheer madness. The second misconstruction is quite the opposite: that I am involved with charitable works. On occasion I receive requests for money, straight up, not from charitable foundations but from Mr. and Mrs. Everybody, generally accompanied by an explanation: "I would like to write a book. You know how it is, so I have to stop working and I'm not rolling in dough," (and I am?). Other misinterpretations: I lack imagination where the content of my novels is concerned, so I feed off my correspondents' secret confessions; or I am in search of sexual partners; or I am desperate to convert to some religion, or to the Internet. And so on.

The truth is both more limited and more mysterious, even to me. I don't know why I answer my mail. I'm not looking for anything or anybody. While I appreciate the fact that people write to me about my books, that is not the only subject that feeds these missives, far from it. When a correspondence develops in a pleasant way—and, thank God, this does happen—I am given to experience the imponderable delight of getting to know someone a little, of reading human words. You don't have to be having withdrawal symptoms to enjoy this sort of contact.

With Melvin Mapple, until only a few weeks earlier, that was how things had been. And perhaps they still were, only I could no longer be sure. I now felt a malaise that defied all analysis. It dated from before the photograph. Seeing him naked had not helped things. Apart from the epiphenomena arising from my vague celebrity, I'm just like anyone else: to have a relationship with someone means that naturally there will be problems. Even when things go well, there are ups and downs, tension, misunderstandings, which may seem harmless at the time, but only five years later will we understand why they made our relation untenable. With Melvin Mapple, it had taken only five months. I wanted to believe that the situation was not irremediable, because he did make me want to have him as a friend.

Five days later I received an answer from the gallery owner in the Marolles:

*Brussels, May 23, 2009*

Dear Amélie,

The photograph of Melvin Mapple is great. To make it clearer to people, I need a picture of him in uniform. Can you ask him for one? Thanks. Talk to you soon,

Albert Cullus

This seemed perfectly normal. I wrote to the American at once, at Cullus's request. I added a P.S. to indicate that I too liked the picture a great deal, with some sort of platitude in the vein of, "It's so interesting to see at last what the person I have been corresponding with actually looks like." If I hadn't said anything at all about the picture, Melvin Mapple might have thought I was rejecting him.

Not long afterwards I went to Brussels to vote. On June 7, there were both European and regional elections. I wouldn't miss an election for anything on earth. In Belgium, it goes without saying, if you don't vote you are punished with a hefty fine. In my case no threats are needed: I would sooner die than fail to fulfill my electoral duty.

Besides, it would be an opportunity to see Brussels again, once my hometown; I don't visit often enough. There is a sweetness to life in Brussels that the denizens of Paris cannot even begin to imagine.

I extended my stay to record a program for Belgian television that would be broadcast in the fall. I took the train back to Paris on the morning of June 10. A great deal of mail had accumulated over three days and was waiting for me on my desk, which meant that I did not immediately notice the absence of a reply from Melvin Mapple. On June 11, I realized that I had sent my last letter to him on May 27 and that such a long silence was unusual, coming from him.

There was no need to be particularly worried. The rhythm of a correspondence can change, that's normal. I myself was not very consistent, and I would raise my eyes to the heavens if one of my correspondents began to panic because of too long a gap between my replies. I would not allow myself to succumb to such a psychosis; I was someone with a certain amount of sangfroid.

One week later, still nothing. The same the following week. I sent a letter repeating the same information as in my letter of May 27: perhaps it had gotten lost.

By mid-July I still had no news of Melvin Mapple, and I was beginning to worry. Did the American soldier think I had failed to show enough interest in his photograph? Such narcissism was not like him. Or perhaps he was finding it difficult to come up with a good portrait of himself as a soldier for Cullus? But we weren't asking for a masterpiece.

With this in mind, I wrote to him right away to tell him that a very simple photograph would suffice. I adopted a friendly tone, and it was sincere: I missed our communication.

No answer. I left on vacation, asking my publisher to forward my mail. I took with me all the American soldier's letters: on rereading them I felt nostalgic. I took note of his companions' names: could I write to Plumpy, or Bozo? They were nicknames, but perhaps it would be enough. So I sent short messages to these two fellows, at the same address, and asked them how Melvin Mapple was doing.

Something must have happened to him. The war was supposed to be over, but on the news there were regular reports of attacks on soldiers based in Iraq. And Melvin was also fighting on another front, that of obesity: perhaps he'd had a stroke, or a heart attack, the kind of accident that happens to hearts that are smothered in fat.

I did not hear from Plumpy, or Bozo, or Mapple. I didn't like the sound of this silence. This was not the first time I'd found myself confronted with such a situation. To be sure, an epistolary relationship is not a contract, you can get out of it whenever you want, without prior notice. I have dropped a few myself when they no longer seemed tenable. And there have also been correspondents who stopped answering me, without an explanation. In most cases I do not get upset, for the simple reason that I do not have time, given the affluence of new letters from strangers.

But occasionally I persisted, when the correspondence had been going on for a long time, and the correspondent was fragile in age or in health. I would phone. Only once did I allow myself to dig deeper: a charming old gentleman in Lyon had not answered my letters in a year and a half, so I took the liberty of asking a young friend of mine in Lyon, whose brother worked in the local administration, to check whether the gentleman had died. The friend did me that favor, and I found out that the man was still alive. More than that I did not know. Any conjecture was possible, from Alzheimer's to the mystical desire to drop all communication.

It is very difficult to know where to stop. Once again there is the problem of barriers: another person goes through your life, and you must agree to have him leave it as easily as he entered. Naturally, you can tell yourself it's not serious, that the connection was no more than an exchange of letters. Or you can also tell yourself that just because you have fallen silent your friendship has not ended for all that. This last argument is more convincing than the previous one. You become wise, you find consolation. You welcome your new friends without forgetting those who have chosen silence. No one is replaceable.

And yet it may come to pass that you wake up in the middle of the night, your heart beating fit to burst: what if that person were in trouble? had been kidnapped by thugs? was overwhelmed by unimaginable worries? Yet how could you, in the name of a certain idea of civilization, have been prepared to abandon him so easily? What is the meaning of such abject coldness?

There is no solution. You must become resigned: you will die without knowing what has happened to your friend, and without knowing whether that friend would have liked you to care about his fate. You will die without knowing whether you are an indifferent bastard or someone who is respectful of another person's freedom. The only thing you will want to go on believing, right to the end, is that this person truly was a friend: why should a friend made of paper and ink be any less precious than a friend made of flesh and blood?

In the summer of 2009 I had not yet reached that stage with Melvin Mapple. I refused to enter the mourning process which I knew so well, however: something in me rebelled against that eventuality. It seemed to me that the conditions were not at all ripe for me to put the mechanisms of resignation in motion. There are limits to how abrupt things can be. This was not irrational on my part: an obese soldier based in Iraq was bound to be in great danger.

After my summer vacation I went back to Paris. My new novel came out and I was overwhelmed, the way I am every fall. September, October, November, and December are grueling months for me, even my publisher cannot imagine how hard I work. And yet not a moment went by without some dark part of my soul eating away at itself over the thought of Melvin Mapple. A man who weighs over four hundred pounds does not disappear just like that.

When it came time to write a Christmas card to my American publisher, after Merry Christmas and Happy New Year I could not help but add an unusual P.S.: "There is this soldier from your army who is based in Baghdad, the one I talked about to the newspapers in Philadelphia, and he's has given no sign of life for some time now. Is there anything I can do?" I would not have dared ask such a question had Michael Reynolds not been the best of men.

Immediately thereafter I received my *Seasons Greetings* from the publisher with an answer to my P.S. in the form of an e-mail address under the words "Missing in action." Good man!

As the Internet is *terra incognita* to me, I enlisted the help of a press attaché to send my request for information regarding Private Melvin Mapple. We received an enigmatic message in return: "Melvin Mapple not known to U.S. Army."

I then had the idea of formulating my request by wording the soldier's name the way it was done on the envelope: a succession of incomprehensible initials with Mapple in the middle, and again a sequence of initials. There was nothing surprising about this. I had corresponded with several French soldiers whose military addresses were equally bizarre, and where the first name was never mentioned. The French army is sometimes known as *la Grande Muette,* the great silent woman; clearly *la Grande Muette* liked to shroud herself in mystery.

This time, the computer replied that on the subject of a certain Howard Mapple based in Baghdad there was nothing to report.

The press attaché asked me if I was satisfied. I did not want to bother her anymore so I said it was fine: "He probably uses his middle name for our correspondence."

To be honest, I didn't know a thing. I did not even know whether this Howard Mapple had anything whatsoever to do with Melvin. There might be more than one American named Mapple. On the off chance, I wrote a letter to this Howard Mapple, at the familiar address in Iraq:

*Paris, January 5, 2010*

Dear Howard Mapple,

Forgive me for disturbing you. I was corresponding with a soldier who is based, like yourself, in Baghdad, Melvin Mapple. I haven't had any news since May 2009.

Do you know him? Could you help me? Thank you very much.

Amélie Nothomb

After ten days or more had gone by, my heart began to beat harder at the sight of an envelope addressed to me, absolutely identical to Melvin Mapple's envelopes, right down to the handwriting. "At last I will find out what happened," I thought, glad we would be resuming our friendship at last. I was in for a shock, to say the least:

*Baghdad, January 10, 2010*

Miss,

I've had enough of your bullshit. I don't owe that asshole Melvin another thing. Write to him in Baltimore, at this address . . .

Now just fuck off and leave me alone.

Howard Mapple

Well, this Howard fellow certainly did not express himself as decorously as Melvin. It was all the more striking in that, apart from his tone, everything was the same—the paper, the envelope, right down to the handwriting, which did not differ one iota from my friend's. Which in itself was not all that surprising: I've often noticed how similar American handwriting can be from one person to the next—at any rate the block lettered handwriting they teach in some schools, and not the cursive handwriting which is bound to be more personal.

In any case, Howard need not worry, I would importune

him no further. Besides, he had given me the most important information: Melvin had gone back to Baltimore, and I even had his address there.

This might be an embryonic explanation for my friend's silence. They must have told him very abruptly that he'd be going home, and he probably had very little time to prepare himself. I could imagine how traumatic it must be for him to find himself back in the US, after six years on the Iraqi front, not to mention seeing his family again, who would be flabbergasted by his obesity.

Poor Melvin must have lapsed into utter dejection. The tragedy of those who have been shipwrecked by life is that instead of opening themselves to others, they withdraw into their suffering and refuse ever to emerge from it. The fact remains that if Melvin had written to me and told me about it, I wouldn't have been able to help him. But at least he could have voiced his feelings, if indeed correspondence can even be said to be a form of speech; confiding in others can rescue you from asphyxia.

Or perhaps in Baltimore Melvin Mapple had found old friends or made new ones, and he no longer needed me. I sincerely hoped as much. But that did not stop me from wanting to have one last communication with this man who, for a brief time, had meant something to me.

I had to find the right tone. It would not even cross my mind to reproach him: everyone has the right to keep silent. Since I myself cannot bear it when others complain about my prolonged silences, it is only fair that I grant the same prerogative to my acquaintances. Moreover, could I hide the fact that I had missed him?

There is only one way to overcome the difficulty of

writing, and that is to write. Thought only becomes effective and productive at the time of writing.

*Paris, January 15, 2010*

Dear Melvin Mapple,

A gentleman by the name of Howard Mapple has informed me that you have gone home and he gave me your address. What a joy it is to have news of you! I must confess I was beginning to get a bit worried, but I can understand that your sudden departure, compounded by the emotion of seeing your family again, must not have left you the time or the receptiveness of mind to write to me.

When you can, would you write me a little letter? I would like so much to find out how you are. The few months we spent corresponding to each other made you important to me. I think of you often. How is Scheherazade?

Best wishes,

Amélie Nothomb

Thus, I mailed what seemed not so much a letter as a message in a bottle.

As a rule, I toss any vulgar correspondence I receive into the wastepaper basket. However, I did not throw out Howard Mapple's letter: I was somewhat intrigued by it, while conceding that its meaning might be perfectly benign. I am in a good position to know that people often say the oddest things in their letters, things that lack any meaning whatsoever. Most people are afraid of seeming too pleasant or of lacking mystery.

Melvin's reply was taking a long time. The Postal Service of the United States Army must be more efficient than the ordinary US Postal Service. I realized I was always making up excuses for the soldier. Had I forgotten that I had found an art gallery for him, that in my role as a confidant I had never let him down? My indulgence toward other people's failings will be the end of me.

I hardly even noticed the ordinary envelope, that day, with its stars and stripes stamp. I stared wide-eyed at the letter I had opened:

*Baltimore, January 31, 2010*

Dear Amélie,

I had decided not to write to you anymore. I am stunned by your letter: how can you not be angry with me?

I expected even worse than reproach. You mean you still haven't realized that I don't deserve your friendship?

    Sincerely,

                            Melvin

    I replied right away:

                      *Paris, February 6, 2010*

Dear Melvin,

    I was so happy to hear from you! Please tell me how things are going for you over there. I've missed you.

    Best wishes,

                            Amélie

    I mailed this note and reread the soldier's short letter. This was the first time he had used my first name on its own, and signed off with his own first name. So I did likewise. His handwriting had changed. That is also why, initially, I hadn't noticed the envelope. Poor Melvin, going home must have really been hard on him: he was letting himself go, he wasn't holding his pen the way he used to, and so on. I was right not to mention it in my reply, that was the appropriate reaction. That way he would know it didn't matter in the least.

    I could just imagine what he must have been going through over these last months. All those idiots finding out he had become obese and saying, "Well, buddy, it seems to have been a rewarding experience. They didn't let you die of hunger." All those bastards blaming him for that disastrous war, when he had been no more than a miserable underling. Human beings can be so revolting when it comes to judging a poor fellow like this! They weren't there, they didn't have to go through the sort of thing he went through, but then they become contrary about things they don't understand at all, and are only too happy to share it with the person in question.

The second envelope from Baltimore:

*Baltimore, February 13, 2010*

Dear Amélie,

If I had known you were this kind of person, I would never have written to you. I was wrong about you. From your books I had assumed you were hard and cynical, the sort or person you can't put one over on. Basically, you are a simple, kind person, you're not pushy. And so right now I could just kick myself.

I've behaved very badly toward you. I've been lying to you from the start. I've never been to Iraq, I've never been a soldier. I just wanted to get you interested in me. I've never been out of Baltimore, where my sole activities are eating and surfing on the Internet.

My brother Howard is a soldier in Baghdad. Years ago I helped him pay back some gambling debts after a time he spent in Las Vegas. Since he still owed me a lot, I persuaded him to copy out the e-mails I sent him and forward them to you as letters. When he got your answers, he scanned them for me.

The hoax wasn't meant to get that far out of hand. I thought I'd send you one or two letters, no more. I didn't expect you to be so enthusiastic, nor did I think I would be. Very soon our correspondence became the most important thing in my life—and I should point out that there isn't much in my life. I didn't feel I could tell you the truth. The situation could have dragged on forever. That's what I wanted.

I knew that someday you would ask me for a photograph. So I sent Howard this picture that is an utterly truthful reproduction of my state, in all its gravity. At the time I did not imagine I would be posing for a Belgian art gallery. I can never thank you enough for what you did in that respect, but your generosity merely served to make my bad conscience even worse. When this Monsieur Cullus wanted a picture of me in uniform, I knew I was cornered.

So I began to negotiate the matter with my brother: could he get me some combat fatigues, size XXXL? At that point Howard blew a fuse. He informed me that he had been charging me five dollars a page (something I knew nothing about), so now he didn't owe me anymore. He added that he was fed up to here with all the crap he'd had to write for me, that he was getting sick of copying stuff that was so lame, that you must really be off your rocker to write back to me. In short, I could no longer count on him.

That's why I stopped writing to you. Yet I could have gone on, I could even have kept up my version of the story. I could have typed out the letters and told you that I had burned my uniform in a symbolic gesture as soon as I got back to Baltimore. But by keeping silent, I was giving a decent end to a squalid story. I would be no more than a memory for you, and you would come to the conclusion that my return to the fold was making me take a long hard look at my life.

So I cut all ties with you. What made it easier was that

my brother no longer forwarded your letters to me; I imagine there were a few of them. I missed our correspondence. However, I was convinced I had to keep silent from now on, in our mutual interest.

Then three weeks ago I got your message. It made no sense: you had found out about Howard and yet you weren't angry with me at all, you wrote in as friendly a manner as ever. Could it be you failed to see the truth, even when it was sticking out a mile? Just to dispel any last illusions, I sent you a handwritten reply, so that the change of handwriting would show you it was a hoax. And then, what do you know, you wrote right back to me, this happy little note, as if you hadn't suspected a thing, despite all the flagrant contradictions in the story.

Rest assured, it doesn't mean I think you're an imbecile. It's a beautiful thing to be so trusting. But I feel bad. I know perfectly well that the commonest of mortals will say that I was trying to take you for a ride, and that I succeeded. Most people will see you, if you'll pardon the expression, as the fall guy. And that was not at all what I intended. To be honest, I don't know what my intention was.

One thing is for sure, I did want to attract your attention. And so I did everything I could. I had read on the Internet that you get tons of letters every day. Since I spend my life on the Internet, I thought this was fascinating, all these paper and ink letters that you were constantly writing and receiving. It seemed, how to put it, so real. And there is so little reality in my life. That is why I wanted so desperately for you to share some of your reality with me. The paradox is that in order to enter into your reality, I had to make a travesty of mine.

And that is where I really hold myself to blame: I underestimated you. I didn't need to lie to you to attract your attention. You would have replied in the same way if I had told you the truth, which is that I am a fat man who has ended up in his parents' tire warehouse in Baltimore.

I would like to ask you to forgive me. But I would understand if you refused.

Sincerely,

Melvin Mapple

I sat there, flabbergasted, for an indefinite length of time, incapable of doing a single thing. Was I annoyed, or angry? No. I had simply reached the ultimate degree of speechlessness.

Ever since I was first published in 1992, I have been exchanging letters with so many different individuals. Statistically, there was bound to be a certain proportion of nutcases among them, and over the years this has proved to be the case. But that someone could go as far as Melvin Mapple—that was something I had never envisaged, not even by a long shot.

How should I react? I had no idea. Should I even react?

In lieu of an answer to my question, there was one thing I felt like doing: writing to Melvin and laying my cards on the table. Which I promptly did.

*February 20, 2010*

Dear Melvin Mapple,

I was so thrown by your letter on February 13 that I can hardly express myself. This might be a knee-jerk reaction but it won't necessarily keep me from a levelheaded response.

You ask me to forgive you. I have nothing to forgive you for. To forgive you would be to assume you had wronged me in some way. Which you have not.

It would seem that in the United States, if I may say so, lying is the quintessential evil. I am, no doubt, very European: lying does not offend me unless it hurts someone. In this case, I cannot see who has been hurt. A few American soldiers might object, and they would probably be right to do so. But that's not any of my business.

You say that people will take me for a fall guy. I don't see things that way. As a human being, I need to see what is there before me. What you showed me in your letters was simply another way of conveying reality. Out of your hell you made another hell. I have no time for the cries of protest of people who will assert that you cannot compare the horror of the Iraqi war with the horror of an obese body—and I quote—"who has ended up in his parents' tire warehouse." This metaphor made sense to you because to you it was vital, and you needed a witness, the sort of person who had impressed you with her steady practice of letter-writing. To see your story written down in ink by a third party was the only way for you to give it the reality it was so cruelly lacking.

You write, "You would have replied in the same way if I had told you the truth." We don't know about that. Yes, I would have replied to you. In the same way? I don't know. You had a lot of nerve, using such a metaphor, but it did have the advantage of showing me, ever so eloquently, how ignominious your life is. If you had told me everything straight out, would I have understood? I hope so.

If this can reassure you, you are by no means the first inveterate liar ever to write to me. And you're not even a true inveterate liar, because you were aware of your invention, so much so that you have become the first person to have voluntarily removed your mask. Of all the people who have written to me, there have been some whose lies were blatantly obvious the moment I started reading their letters, others whose trickery took me as long as four years to detect, and still others whose stunt I have not yet discovered. Besides, to get back to what I said at the beginning of my letter, as long as it does not hurt anyone, inveterate lying does not bother me in the least.

I would also like to congratulate you: your scheme was so clever I was in no danger of ever finding out, had you not confessed. Well done. There is a crook in every writer, so I take my hat off to you as a colleague. When an untalented inveterate liar tries to ensnare me with a blatant falsehood, I feel afflicted. Fraud, like the violin, demands perfection: for a violinist to give a recital it is not enough for him to be good. He must be sublime or nothing. And in you, I am saluting a master.

Sincerely,

Amélie Nothomb

Without realizing, I had used his "sincerely" to end my letter. And indeed, in this letter, I had displayed a rare sincerity. My only omission was that I had been annoyed by his "I did want to attract your attention." How often have I read this sentence? And it is such a pleonasm. If you're writing to someone, it's because you want to attract their attention. Otherwise, you wouldn't write to them.

But this could be excused because for once it didn't come with the sentence which follows that formula nine times out of ten: "I couldn't bear it if you treated me like everyone else." There are numerous variations on this nonsense: "I'm not like other people," "I wouldn't like for you to speak to me as if I were just anybody," and so on. The moment I read this sort of thing, I throw the letter in the wastepaper basket. To obey their injunction. You don't want me to treat you like everyone else? Your wish is my command. I have the deepest respect for everyone. You are asking for exceptional treatment, therefore I shall not respect you, I shall throw your epistle into the wastebasket.

What I cannot stand about this statement, other than the fact that it is stupid, is that it is oozing with contempt. Contempt that is all the more reprehensible in that it has been ascribed to me. It is something I am absolutely allergic to, I cannot stand any form of contempt, whether it has been addressed to me, imputed to me, or I have simply been a witness thereof. As for holding everyone in contempt, that is even more revolting. It is simply inadmissible not to grant a stranger the benefit of the doubt.

I've had gingerbread with honey. I love the taste of honey. The word "sincere," so fashionable nowadays, takes its etymology from "*sine cera*," literally "without wax," which is a reference to purified honey, of a superior quality—for there was a time when swindlers would sell you a nasty mixture of honey and wax. All those people who misuse the word "sincerity" nowadays ought to have some good honey therapy to remind themselves whereof they speak.

*Baltimore, February 27, 2010*

Dear Amélie,

I was even more stunned by your letter than you must have been by mine. I don't know what I expected but certainly not that.

I think your reaction was very beautiful. The only other person who knew about my lie was my brother Howard. He doesn't share your tolerance, to say the least. When I was sending him the e-mails to copy out for you, he would greet them with a "God you are such a sicko" or some other equally refined expression.

Go figure: you're not blaming me, and as a result I feel in the wrong. I feel I need to justify myself, but you're not even asking me to.

What I told you about my life until I turned thirty is the truth: drifting, sleeping rough, poverty, and finally hunger. But when I touched bottom I didn't join the army, I went home to Mom and Dad. It was a hell of a humiliation to go back to living with my parents at the age of thirty, without a single accomplishment to my name. My mother thought by buying me a computer she was rescuing me. "You can design a website for our gas station," she said. As if a gas station needs a website! I could smell her pretext a mile off. But I had no choice, so I set to work. I found out that I wasn't too bad at this line of work. A few local businesses asked me to do their websites, too. I made some money, which allowed me to bail Howard out of debt.

In fact, that was my undoing. I had just spent ten years doing nothing but walking and starving; now, switch those verbs to their opposites and there I am adopting the lifestyle of a programmer—never using my legs and snacking all day long. My impression that my mother had given me that computer for me to redeem myself was so strong that I didn't leave the screen for an entire year. I did not stop except to sleep, wash, or share a family meal—more eating, again. My parents could not see beyond the version of the scrawny son who had returned to the fold; they didn't notice I was putting on weight and neither did I. I should have looked at myself in the shower, but I didn't pay any attention. By the time I realized the extent of the disaster—and that's the word for it—it was too late.

If there is one ailment where prevention is better than cure, it's obesity. To notice that you have ten or even twenty pounds to lose, that's nothing. But to find out one fine day that you've got sixty pounds to lose is something else altogether. And yet, if I had started even then, I could have saved myself. Now I have two hundred and ninety pounds to lose. Who has the courage to try to lose two hundred and ninety pounds?

Why didn't I ring the alarm bells when I found out I was sixty pounds overweight? I had some thorny computer problems that day, and I needed all my energy and concentration: no way could I start thinking about a diet. The next day was the same, and on it went. The mirror confirmed the verdict of the scales: I was fat. But I swore that it didn't matter: who was looking at me? I was a programmer, I lived in my parents' tire warehouse with a computer that didn't give a damn how much I weighed. I put on a sweat suit and an XXL T-shirt and you couldn't tell. At mealtimes neither my father nor my mother noticed a thing.

When I was walking across America, like any self-respecting Kerouac wannabe, I tried the drugs that were available on the road and in the desert, which meant a lot of drugs. Your buddies always have some substance in their pocket: "Share the experience," they tell you as they hand you some. I never turned it down. Some stuff I liked, other stuff I hated. But even the drugs I really got hooked on never amounted to one-hundredth of the addiction to food I suffered from. When I see anti-drug campaigns on television I wonder what they're waiting for to warn us against our true enemy.

That's why I can't even begin to lose weight: my dependency on food has become invincible. It would take a straitjacket, size XXXL, to stop me eating.

When I hit two hundred and seventy, my mother said to me, stunned, "You're fat!" I replied that I was obese. "Why haven't I noticed anything until now?" she cried. Because I'd let my beard grow, and it hid my triple chin. I shaved it off and discovered the face of a stranger, the stranger I still am.

My parents ordered me to lose weight. I refused. "If that's the way you want it, we won't have you at the dinner table anymore. We don't want to be witnesses to your suicide," they said. And so I became a solitary fat man. It didn't bother me not to see my father and mother anymore. In the end, that's what's so awful: nothing bothers you, you can accept everything. You think, no way will I ever become obese, because that would be unbearable: it is unbearable, but you bear it.

I'm at a point where I don't see anyone anymore, other than the deliveryman who brings me the food I order over the phone or the Internet, and nothing fazes him: he's probably seen it all, in Baltimore. I put my dirty laundry in a garbage bag; when it's full, I put it outside the garage door. My mother washes it, then brings the bag back to the same place. That way she doesn't have to look at me.

In the fall of 2008, I read an article about rising rates of obesity among American soldiers based in Iraq. In the beginning I thought it was my brother Howard who should have put on weight and not me. Then I began to envy those obese soldiers. What I mean is that they at least had a real excuse to be fat. Their status made them seem like victims. Some people might say it wasn't their fault. I was jealous, because they had people feeling sorry for them. It's pathetic, I know.

But that's not everything. There was a history behind their pathology. And I envied them for that, too. You'll tell me that mine has a history, too: well, maybe it does, but I don't know what it is. According to the facts, there was a cause for my obesity and yet in my mind there was no connection to the laws of causality. Living full-time on the Internet creates such a sensation of unreality that it's as if all the food I had been devouring for months had never existed. I was a fat man without a history and as such I was jealous of those who had been incorporated into History with a capital H.

When the war in Iraq began, they contacted me and declared me unfit due to obesity—already! At the time, I was

glad I was fat and I thought it was hilarious that my idiot
brother got sent over there. And so my nothingness in front
of the computer continued: eight years of nothing, with
nothing to show for it in my memory, and yet I couldn't just
forget those eight years, since they had burdened me with
over two hundred pounds. Then I read the article about
the obese soldiers. And you came into the picture.

It was the conjunction of that newspaper article and the
discovery of your existence that gave me the idea for my
lie. For a start I'd been intrigued by the idea of a novelist
who writes to her readers on real stationery. I ordered your
books translated into English and although I can't say why,
they really struck a chord with me. You'll probably be
annoyed, but it was one of your characters who gave me
the idea for my lie, the young Christa in *Antichrista*.

Suddenly this new interpretation of my obesity began
to seem like my salvation. For my version to become real,
it had to receive a stamp of approval from someone outside. You were perfect for the part: well-known, and
responsive. I don't know if corresponding with you did me
good, but I do know I really enjoyed it: you were assuring
me of a history. I had really begun to believe that I was a
soldier in Baghdad. Thanks to you, I had something I have
never had: dignity. In your mind, my life took shape.
Through your gaze, I felt myself exist. My fate was deserving of your consideration. After eight years of nothingness
suddenly I was experiencing incredible emotion and
delight. Even if your letters only reached me in scanned
versions, they seemed so terribly real.

I would have liked for things to go on like that forever,
but you wanted to see a photograph of me in uniform.
And then in the summer of 2009 newspapers the world

over announced the withdrawal of our troops. Howard, with his usual rotten luck, was in the last contingent; he only got back to the US ten days or so ago. In short, when I realized that I could no longer go on with the lie, the only solution was silence.

I got Howard to send me all your letters. It was so moving to see them for real, to touch them. I printed out my own letters, which I had archived, and put together a file with our successive messages. Do you know what I called the folder? "Life Form." It came to me instinctively. When I think back about the dozen months or so spent corresponding with you, and I remember that before that I had had no life at all for nearly ten years, these words suddenly seemed incredibly important: thanks to you, I was now granted a life form.

In theory, life form can refer to the elementary existence of amoebas and protozoa. For most people, that brings to mind a sort of disgusting swarming, nothing more. For someone like me who is familiar with the void, even that in itself is life, and so I must respect it. I loved that life form and I am nostalgic for it. Writing back and forth worked as a kind of fission: I would send you a tiny particle of life, you would read it and make it double, your answer would multiply it, and so on and so forth. Thanks to you, my void was being filled by a little culture of fluid. I was marinating in a sauce of shared words. There was a voluptuous delight in this that nothing could equal: the illusion of having meaning. The fact that this meaningfulness stemmed from a lie did not in any way detract from its delight.

Our correspondence has just resumed after an interruption that lasted as long as its reign. Will it be as good as before? And now that I have told you the truth, will it give rise to a new life form? I'm not at all sure. How can you trust me now? Even supposing that out of the goodness of your soul you could go on writing to me, something has been broken inside me: I was never able to forget that I was lying, and yet I loved the conviction that writing this lie brought to me. You are a writer, you know this only too well. But I'm a neophyte, and I can't get over it: the most intense thing I have ever experienced is something I owe to the shared fiction of which I am the author.

And now my fiction has been demolished. You know the appalling truth. Even the best kept prisoner on the planet can escape. But no escape is possible when the prison is your own obese self. Lose weight? LOL. I weigh nearly four hundred and fifty pounds. Why not deconstruct the pyramids of Egypt, while we're at it?

So let me ask you this: what do I have left to live for?

Sincerely,

Melvin Mapple

The conclusion to his epistle upset me greatly. Melvin's dementia must have been contagious because I immediately bought a plane ticket to Washington. The international operator found me Mapple's phone number without too much difficulty. Allowing for the time difference, I dialed his number. A breathless voice answered, "Is that really Amélie Nothomb?"

"You ran to pick up the phone, didn't you?"

"No. It's next to me. I can't get over the fact you're calling."

Melvin spoke as if he were constantly out of breath. It must have been due to his obesity.

"I land in Washington on March 11 at 2:30 P.M.. I want to see you."

"You're coming for me? I'm very touched. I'll meet you at the airport. Then we'll take the train to Baltimore."

I hung up, afraid I might change my mind. As I have a prodigious talent for recklessness, I ordered myself not to think about the trip anymore, so that I couldn't decide not to go through with it.

Melvin's voice had sounded joyful over the telephone.

J ust as I was about to leave, I received a letter from the American. I took it with me to read on the plane.

I waited for the Boeing 747 to take off, so I could no longer run away, then I opened the envelope:

*March 5, 2010*

Dear Amélie,

You're coming to see me. This is an extraordinary gift. I don't think you do this for all your correspondents, all the more so when they live so far away. What am I going on about? I know you've never traveled this far for anyone else. I'm very touched.

At the same time, I wonder what I wrote that made you decide to come. Without realizing, I might have maneuvered in such a way as to make you feel sorry for me, and I'm not very proud of that. Well, what's done is done. I'm happy.

As I told you on the telephone, I will come to meet you at the Ronald Reagan Airport. I'd like you to know that this will be an extraordinary event for me. I haven't been out of Baltimore in nearly ten years. And when I say out of Baltimore, I should say, to be more precise, out of my street. And even that isn't really accurate. My last raid outside the tire warehouse dates back to President Obama's election, on November 4, 2008: it was to go and vote. Fortunately the polling place was at the end of the street. Still, it nearly killed me, I came home dripping in sweat, as if there were a heat wave on. The worst of it isn't the effort of walking, it's the other people staring at you—that's what makes you sweat. Yes, the epidemic of obesity in America has not yet dissuaded other people from staring. When will we have a president who weighs three hundred pounds?

In short, going to meet you in Washington will be an expedition. Please don't think I'm complaining, that would be out of line, when you are crossing a whole ocean to come and see me. Simply, I want you to know that I am aware of the importance of this event. Nothing on earth will stop me from being at the airport on March 11 at 2:30 P.M.. You've seen my photograph, so you'll recognize me.

You didn't say how long you are staying. I hope it will be a long time. I've asked my mother to make up my old room in case you want to stay at my place.

I'm waiting for you.

Sincerely,

Melvin Mapple

I thought this was a very good letter. I liked the way he said, "Without realizing, I might have maneuvered in such a way as to make you feel sorry for me," which was a change from the endless "I hope you don't think I'm trying to make you feel sorry for me" that some of my correspondents put at the end of their sagas, when they tell me how their parents beat and tortured them when they were little.

As usual, I managed to get myself a window seat. When

traveling by plane I always have my nose up against the window: even the tiniest cloud catches my interest. But this time I didn't manage to lose myself in the contemplation of the celestial landscape. My brain had a pebble in its shoe.

Halfway across the Atlantic, this mental pebble managed to find a voice: "Amélie Nothomb, can you tell me what you are doing?" Most hypocritically I replied, "Well, when all is said and done, I am a responsible adult who has decided to go and visit an American friend." "An unlikely story! The truth is you haven't changed since you were eight years old: you think you have been endowed with mysterious powers, you imagine you will touch Melvin and he will be cured of his obesity!" I blocked my ears, but the voice continued. "Of course! I hadn't quite found the words for it, with you speech is rational, it's what's underneath that is not rational, but you think you're going to save Mapple, even if you don't know how you're going to go about it. Why else would you be going all the way to the United States just to see a simple correspondent?" "Because I feel an affinity for this man who, at least, does not indulge in paraleipsis." "You are crossing the Atlantic for an absence of paraleipsis? What a laugh!" "No. It is the rarest of virtues, an absence of paraleipsis. I am capable of going a very long way in the name of my semantic convictions. Language, for me, is the highest degree of reality." "The highest degree of reality is that you are about to meet an obese inveterate liar in a tire warehouse in Baltimore. A dream companion for a dream destination. All for the sake of an absence of paraleipsis. If someday you happen upon a correspondent from Outer Mongolia who is the only one of his kind not to make mistakes in the use of the possessive apostrophe, or who might even have an interesting take on the illocutionary conditional, will you go and visit him in Ulan Bator?" "What is the point of all this rhetorical clowning?" "And you, what is the point of this trip of yours? What makes you think your miraculous presence will help that poor lunatic? If he wants to do something about it, which is not at all a given, you're not the one who can get him out of the fix he's in. If it were simply a matter of wasting your time, it wouldn't be so serious. But have you given any thought to how uncomfortable you are going to feel around him? You had things to write to each other, granted; what will you have to say to each other? You will be faced with hours of silence with this fat man, first at the airport, then during a long train ride, then in a taxi, and finally at his house. It's going to be hell. Given the absence of conversation, you won't be able to avoid staring at his fat, and if he realizes, you are both going to suffer. Why inflict this on yourself, and why inflict it on him?" "It might not be like that at all." "No, of course not, it might be even worse. You are about to meet a programmer who in ten years has spoken to no one but the pizza deliveryman. When you get to Baltimore, he will feel so bad that he will sit in front of his computer so he won't have to deal with you. The man is sick and you are even sicker because you're going to his house. You've gotten yourself in one hell of a mess. Well, now you'll have to deal with it, you pathetic idiot."

The pitiless voice fell silent, leaving me with the implacable realization of my mistake. Yes, this trip was a calamitous idea, I was fully aware of that now. What could I do? There was no going back. How could I stop the plane from reaching its destination? How could I get out of the airport through a different gate from the one where Melvin Mapple would be waiting for me? It was impossible!

The flight attendant was handing out the pale green forms that are mandatory for anyone about to step onto American soil, even for three hours. When people see these forms for the first time, they never fail to be astonished by the questionnaire they have to answer: "Have you ever been or are you now involved in terrorist activities?"; "Do you have any chemical or nuclear weapons in your possession?" and other astonishing questions, with boxes for ticking yes or no. These neophytes burst out laughing and say to their traveling companions: "What will happen if I tick yes?" There is always someone who will firmly dissuade them: "You don't mess around with security in the United States." Which means that in the end, even the most foolhardy resist the temptation.

I knew these green forms by heart and I was ready to fill them out as usual when I had a sudden idea: "Amélie, the only way for you to avoid meeting Melvin Mapple is to tick the wrong boxes. You will be handed over to the American justice system. Which do you prefer? The train from Washington to Baltimore with an obese inveterate liar, or major hassles with the American legal system?"

Never in my life have I set myself such an ultimatum. I looked out the window at the haunted sky, which already knew the answer. I had made my decision, it was beyond reflection. Ecstatic, I committed the insane deed. To the question, "Have you ever been involved in terrorist activities?" I ticked yes. A whirling impression. To the question, "Do you have any chemical or nuclear weapons in your possession?" I ticked yes. Profound stupefaction. And so on. In a trance, my mind wide open, I ticked yes yes yes, each tick more suicidal than the next. I signed a deed of self-incrimination which transformed me into global public enemy number one and I slipped it into my passport.

At this stage nothing was irreversible. I could still call the flight attendant and ask for a new green questionnaire, the way people do when they have crossed things out. All I had to do was tear up the insane deposition and it would have no further consequences.

But I knew that I would do no such thing. I knew I would give my demented document to the customs official. What would happen after that, I didn't exactly know, other than that I would have awe-inspiring problems. The authorities would send me to Guantánamo. There are rumors that this Gehenna is being closed down, but Americans are nothing if not efficient: you can be sure they have built another one just like it somewhere else. I would be stuck in prison until the end of my days.

All this just to avoid meeting Melvin Mapple? Fiddlesticks! Amélie, you are following your destiny, something you have always wanted. Punishment for your numerous sins? There's some of that there, too. But that's not half of it.

What has your quest been, ever since you started writing? What have you been lusting after for so long, with such irrepressible determination? What exactly is writing for you?

You know what it is: if every day of your life you write like a woman possessed, it is because you need an emergency exit. For you, being a writer means desperately seeking the way out. An adventure that was the fault of your recklessness has brought you to that way out. Stay on the plane, wait until you get there. You'll hand your documents over to customs. And your impossible life will be over. You will be delivered from your biggest problem, which is yourself.